THE PANTY RIPPER

2

Introducing Becky Nash

A NOVEL

GODREALITY WAY

Good 2 Go Publishing

Copyright © 2015 by Good2Go Publishing

ISBN: 9780990869467

Published 2015 by Good2Go Publishing
7311 W. Glass Lane, Laveen, AZ 85339
www.good2gopublishing.com
Twitter @good2gobooks
G2G@good2gopublishing.com
Facebook.com/good2gopublishing
ThirdLane Marketing: Brian James
Brian@good2gopublishing.com

Cover Design: Davida Baldwin

Printed in the United States of America

Acknowledgments

Thank you everyone for your support. Enjoy!

THE PANTY RIPPER
2

1 Chap

Omar Goodness sat behind his cherry oak wood desk at his Goodies warehouse, skimming through fabrics that were imported from India while waiting on Becky Nash, a potential intern, who just so happened to be an hour late. The time lapsed; his mind began to drift off to its favorite subject "TIA FIELDS." Omar was still secretly in contact with her mom Miss Fields so he had firsthand knowledge of Tia's day-to-day agenda.

Omar's thoughts were interrupted by a light knock on his office door. "Come in," he shouted. The door opened and in walked Becky Nash, his newest intern. Becky was as white as a snowflake and extremely beautiful, in a soap opera kind of way. "Good morning Miss. Nash, have a seat please."

"Good morning Mr. Goodness," Becky's voice was powerful and yet seductive at the same time.

"Well, I've looked over your references and it seems that you are over-qualified for the position Miss. Nash."

"Mr. Goodness, I would like, totally be ecstatic if you were my boss. I've been nothing but an avid supporter of your Goodies line of lingerie and I personally want to take it to another level of sexy intertwined with class." Becky's words were starting to get a rise out of Omar. To him, nothing was sexier than elevating Goodies to another level. Becky was also in her thoughts. She had a secret fetish for black men that she had never actually fulfilled. "If given this position Mr. Goodness, I promise to give you one hundred percent of Becky Nash!"

Omar lifted his head from her resume with a raised eyebrow, "Oh, I apologize…that did not come out right. What I am trying to say is… I'll put one hundred percent of hard work and dedication into advancing what you have already built Mr. Goodness." It was something about the way that she said "Mr. Goodness" that was causing Omar to fantasize about ripping Becky Nash panties off and bending her over the top of his desk. He could actually see it in his mind.

Omar got up and locked his office door. *"So Miss Nash,"* he says while folding his arms, his right hand raised, rubbing his chin in contemplation, *"you say that you can do the job well?"*

"I can like totally show you better than I can tell you ...how about we start in the department of oral services Mr. Goodness."

"Let's," was his only response. Omar strode across the room with a hunger in his eyes that causes Becky to cream herself instantly. Aggressively, he spun her chair around as he stared down into her ocean blue eyes. Becky removed her hairpins that held her long blond hair in a bun, causing it to cascade down her back and over her shoulders. Omar loosened his belt and let his slacks drop down to his ankle; with the skill of a porn star she grabs hold of Omar's erection, licks her lips

then spits directly on his cock as she strokes his shaft ferociously.

"Is everything okay Mr. Goodness?" "Mr. Goodness?" Becky asked with a flirtatious flattering concern breaking Omar out of his deep, erotic daydream

"Oh excuse me, a million, and one things on my mind," he lied. "So... I'll see you tomorrow at 9 a.m. Miss Nash." his intoxicating smile caused more leakage between her legs.

"9 a.m. sharp!" she responded with a flirtatious smile.

Becky Nash

"Can you like freaking' believe it? I actually landed the internship at Goodes and was personally interviewed by the smoking hot Omar Goodness...

can you believe my luck Kelly!" Becky screamed excitedly to her best friend.

"Wow! I'm totally stoked for you." Kelly replied sarcastically, jealous of her best friend Becky who seemed to always upstage her effortlessly since they were in grade school.

"Don't be such a buzz kill, and I'll consider letting you be my maid of honor."

Kelly cracked up laughing at her friend who she felt was clearly delusional, "and what makes you believe that a self-made millionaire like Omar Goodness will ever consider marrying a skank like you?" She teased.

"Has not every man that I have known dropped down to one knee and offered me the world?"

"Never out of love... you kinky-little whore bag."

Becky licked her lips slowly and confidently responds "So not true. I mean, they love the things that I do…"

"And the things that you let them to do to you."

Becky smiled "And trust me…Omar Goodness will be no different!"

Bria

Brianna Jones was still on her mission to ensure that Tia Fields would never give Omar Goodness the satisfaction of making any type of amends with her. Bria was convinced that Omar had set her up with Malika (Millie), obtained the explicit photos, and then threatened to turn them over to Tia. So now, it was her turn to play shady and she had the perfect plan to do so.

"So this is where all the Goodness happens," Bria said as she patted her hand a couple of times on Joy's bed. Joy was oblivious to the fact that she was being played and her ear-to-ear smile proved it.

"Yup!" Joy exclaimed. "If this bed could talk, it would scream Omar Goodness louder than I ever have." Joy did not have a problem with talking to Bria about Omar now that Bria crossed over and was a proud, full-blown lesbian.

"That good huh?"

"Yup, the best I ever had."

"Well now you're going to have it even when he is not around." Bria pilled the nanny cam teddy bear out and placed it on Joy's dresser. "Joy, if anyone would have told me that you were this freaky behind closed doors I would have called them a liar."

Joy smiled "girl, you don't even know the half...maybe I'll teach you a trick or two."

"Good, because I really need to step my shit up to get my baby girl Tia back."

2 Chap

Tia

Tia Fields had finally passed the Bar exam, allowing her to be practice criminal law. Today was her graduation ceremony and excited was an understatement to describe the way that she felt at that very moment. She had just left the stage where she had received her diploma and was all smiles as she made her way back to her seat.

"Congratulations Miss Fields," Thomas Wingate said cutting off Tia's path. Thomas was what one would consider the definition of "arrogant" and not a soul could convince him that Tia would not be his wife and the mother to his children. He chased her all throughout, only to be rejected each and every time.

"Thanks Thomas, congrats to you as well," Tia said as she tried to side step him, unsuccessfully.

You do know I can get you a great position at my dad's firm. It's only the biggest firm in America."

Tia gave Thomas the (are you serious) look. "Well if that's the case then your dad's firm will be my competition, and you know what I do to the competition Mr. Wingate." Tia smiled, sidestepped Thomas, and headed back to her seat feeling like a million bucks; *no more paralegal s*he thought with the biggest smile on her face.

Tia walked out of the ceremony to the surprise of her life. She thought her eyes were playing tricks on her but they were not. Omar Goodness stood in front of a horse and carriage wearing a white tuxedo, holding a bouquet of flowers.

"Can somebody please recommend me to a good lawyer?" he screamed out flashing his radiant smile. Tia's heart skipped a beat but she decided to play along.

"And what kind of trouble are you in sir?"

"Well I have been falsely accused of being a heartbreaker."

Tia did not want to laugh but she could not help herself. "Boy you know you crazy right... and guilty as charged."

Omar reached his hand out to her, "come take a ride with me." Tia was a little apprehensive at first but thinking *what the hell,* she reached for Omar's hand and let him lead her onto the carriage.

The night air was pleasant as they rode the first few minutes in silence. Tia stared up at the stars thinking about the promising career that she was about to embark on, while Omar thought nothing other than marriage. "So does this mean that I am forgiven?"

Tia shot Omar the *corner of the eye look,* you know the one where she does not turn her head, but shifted her eyeballs to the corner. Omar raised both hands in defense, "too soon huh?"

"You think?" She says sarcastically but blatantly. "Let's just enjoy the good things of this day instead picking at old ugly wounds."

"Ok, you're right... So are you hungry because I can eat a house?"

And the hell out of a pussy. She thought. "Sure, what do you have in mind?"

"Strawberries and whip cream," he joked.

"Yeah, I bet you do. But no, seriously."

Omar smiled grabbed Tia's hand and said, *"It's a surprise."*

Ramona's

Ramona's was the best Italian restaurant in town. The food was five-star, remarkable, and the service was just as great. Their meals were done and now Omar and Tia were half way through an expensive bottle of vintage wine.

"Let's toast," Omar exclaimed raising his glass. Tia raised her glass and started into his enticing eyes. "Here's to never given up until you get what you desire."

One hour later, the horse and carriage pulled up to the front of Tia's home. They climbed down and walked to her front door. "Well thanks to adding on to my already amazing day." She said as she placed her back against the door. Omar was crushed, but he was a fighter so he quickly countered

"Why stop at amazing where we can make it a night that we'll never forget."

"Good night Omar... it's already a night that I'll never forget, I passed the Bar, remember?" Omar saw the window of opportunity closing quickly but he still gave it one last try.

"Can I come in for a minute; I can really use a glass of water?"

"I do not have any bottled water and my pipes are rusted." She lied with the cutest smile.

"Well can I use the bathroom real quick?"

"The toilet's broke."

"Can I fix it?"

Tia burst out laughing. Omar was pouring it on thick but not thick enough.

"Go home Omar." Omar put on a sad little puppy dog face and said, "Ok, goodnight Mrs. Fields."

Tia grabbed him by his shirt, pulling him into her, "Come here." She stuck her sweet tongue down Omar's throat, and then sucked on his bottom lip. Omar's inner beast took control as he began to ravage her mouth with his lethal tongue. He viciously flicked it in and out of her mouth sending shivers down her spine and war juices down her inner thigh. Tia pushed Omar back and gasped. "Damn, they need to put that thing in a cage." she said referring to his tongue.

"Let me in Tia... I wanna suck that pussy to sleep. I want you to ride this dick for the rest of our lives."

"Maybe I'll think about it if you can keep your nose clean and your dick in your pants. But until then, I have a little gift for you." She grabbed Omar's hand and placed it under her skirt and on her silk panties. "Would you like to take these home with you, they are drenched?"

"Can I please?" Omar begged. The feeling of the damp silk fabric against his fingertips drove him wild.

"Well I'm not going to take them off and hand them to you so how are you going to get them?" The words barely left Tia's mouth when she heard the first tear of the fabric. "Ooooh get em baby." Then there was another rip. "Yes...Yes, Omar, take it..." Then there was a yank, another rip, and a growl that came from Omar's mouth.

He had successfully panty ripped her and now he was backpedaling to the horse and carriage rubbing her wet panties against his nose. Tia was ready to say *the hell with it*, and drag Omar's ass back into her home; but instead, she went alone, raced to her nightstand, pulled out the plumber, and buzzed herself to multiple squirting orgasms, all the while screaming for Omar Goodness to fuck her harder.

3 Chap

The Intern

Becky Nash walked through the Goodies factory micromanaging and critiquing the new patterns and designs. For the most part Becky felt that they were good but not great and she had a few ideas that she wanted to run by Omar, so she headed to his office.

Becky entered into Omar's office and her mouth instantly began to water. Boy does she want to taste that chocolate. "How can I help you Miss Nash?"

He asked without taking his eyes off of his computer screen.

"I'm here to make a formal recommendation." She replied sweetly.

"I'm listening," with his eyes still locked on his screen.

"Well I think if we added a pinch of kinky to the Goodies brand; our sales will triple over the winter."

"Kinky?" She now had Omar's full attention as he lifted his head with raised eyebrows.

"Yes... I was thinking along the lines of leather and latex."

"Whoa!" Omar exclaimed. "I have to be honest Miss Nash, I--"

"Please, call me Becky."

"Okay Becky look, I run a very classy operation here at Goodies and I'm not sure of what type of image I would be portraying with a leather and latex line."

"Mr. Goodness, let me be the first to tell you that, the some of the classiest woman in America have a leather and latex fetish." Becky says with a hint of seduction.

"I'm not sure if that's accurate in the urban market which represents 70% of my consumers…I make sexy affordable."

"Yes, most woman whether urban or suburban, wants to feel sexy. But then there are those nights where we want to feel like a dirty little whore. I'm not sure if you have experienced this in your lifetime Mr. Goodness…" *Omar's mind quickly drifted to Joy and her sex crazed antics.* "Can I ask you a personal question boss?"

"Sure, go ahead."

"Have you ever been with a white woman Mr. Goodness?" Her question totally caught Omar off guard. "I mean like, sexually?"

"No…I haven't."

"That figures."

"Excuse me?"

"My best friend in college was African America and we conversed a lot about the difference between sex and pleasure."

"Didn't know there was a difference. But what does all of this have to do with leather and latex?"

"Given the opportunity to run this new line, I will show you that there are different levels--"

"Different levels to what Becky?" Omar cut her off.

"Of wealth." She countered. "You see, leather and latex will make you a billionaire...And I will personally show you the difference between sex and the ultimate pleasure." She says to the man that previously licked two different women to the emergency room."

"Becky Nash, have you ever been with a black man...sexually?"

"No, but--"

"Let me tell you something Becky, I put the big "O" in "O.M.G. But unfortunately for you, I do not mix business with pleasure."

"Mr. Goodness, trust me when I tell you...you do not have the slightest clue as to what real pleasure feels like. I'll break you down, then build you back up, don't you know that I've been like totally waiting for this moment all of my life."

At that moment, Omar could hear Tia's demands echoing in his head, *"Keep your nose clean and your dick in your pants."* But the job that the intern was working on him was showing good quality.

"Mr. Omar Goodness...leather and latex is about to have the whole damn world screaming GOODNESS GRACIOUS! Including me!" Becky winked and then left the office.

4 Chap

The Fellas

It had been a while since Omar had the chance to hang out with his boys Askari and Kinard, and boy did have a lot to catch them up with. "So you finally got Tia back huh?" Askari asked as sipped on his Cîroc.

"I wouldn't say that I got her back, but we did have a good time together."

"What the hell is a *'good time'*? Did you mash that potato this time or did she fake another seizure after you ate the twat all night?" Askari teased, causing him and Kinard to bust out laughing.

"Ha Ha Ha…real funny. And I don't know why the 40-year-old virgin is over there laughing." Omar quipped as he pointed at Kinard.

"Whatever bro, for you information, I have a lady, and she is a beautiful black queen." Kinard shot back with conviction.

"What did we tell you about claiming chicks on the internet, chicks that you never even met in person?" Omar joked.

"This is why I don't tell you fools anything, because y'all swear a brother be lying…but believe what y'all want. My lady is the bomb and the sex is amazing." Omar and Askari bust out laughing, not believing a word that Kinard was saying.

"But on a more realistic note," Omar, putting his drink down and getting serious. "I have this new intern at Goodies and she basically threw the coochie at me. Now y'all do know that I never mix business with pleasure, but Becky is very intriging."

"Becky!" Kinard screams. "Is she white?"

"Yup, certified snow bunny...with a nice plump wooty."

"And what the hell is a *'wooty'*?" Kinard asked in disgust.

"A *'wooty'*... is a white girl with a booty."

"Wait! Now you know I'm the king of snow bunnies, so let me give you some advice before you lose your damn mind. No matter how good the head is, do not put her in your will because she'll try to kill you in your sleep; then spend the insurance money on plastic surgery." Askari says jokingly but seriously.

"Please do not tell us that you are selling out on us black man. You know, with the success of Goodies and all, it would be real typical for you to marry a white woman." Kinard's snide remark went right over Omar's head because he was not going to entertain it.

"The only reason I refuse to show her that there is good and there's goodness, is the fact that Tia's going to give me a chance to prove to her that I am not the low down dirty dog that she thinks I am."

"Wow! Omar Goodness is finally going to be a man and do the right thing." Kinard applauded but not without adding, "Let's see how long that lasts."

Love of His Life

Kinard rang the doorbell twice. In his hand were two dozen long stem roses. The door swung open and there stood the love his life. She was wearing the most innocent of attire; a pleated dress that came down past her knees, and a cashmere sweater that she normally would not be caught dead in.

"Hello my queen, these are for you." He said as he handed her the roses.

"Kinard, you shouldn't have... you are spoiling me baby." Joy grabbed the roses and Kinard's hand, led him into the house, and straight up the stairs to her bedroom. "So now it's time for me to spoil you back." Joy said as she pushed him onto the bed.

"Wow...what's gotten into you?" Kinard asked with an excitedly aroused tone. Having a woman take control was something he had only heard about when listening to Omar and Askari talk about their many sexcapades. Instead of responding to him, Joy

snatched his belt off, then his pants, and finally his

briefs. She then grabbed a bottle of chocolate syrup

from the side of the bed and began to put it all over

his dick and balls. Kinard could not even believe

that this was actually happening until she took him

into her hot mouth, *"ummmmm"* (slurp…slurp),

"you taste…" (Slurp…slurp) "…so damn good

baby…" Joy knew exactly what she was doing and

why she was doing it, and for the next 45 seconds,

she ate Kinard alive until he flooded her throat.

"ARRRRRRRRGGH," he screamed as his toes

curled into a fist. Kinard could barely talk and

hardly open his eyes but he could feel her milking

him for every single drop. (PLOOP), Joy finally let

him out of that "head lock" while stroking out the

rest of his cum causing him to squirm each time her

hand came up and caressed his very sensitive dick tip.

"Are you okay?" She asked, with a devilish smile knowing that she had just put that work in on him. Kinard nodded his head faster than a bobble head doll. He wanted to ask her where the hell was all that cum that he just shot into her mouth, but it was obvious that she just swallowed it all. This was the first time he had experienced that and it simply blew his mind.

"I...I...I...love you!" He stuttered with tears welling up in his eyes. Joy knew that she had him right where she wanted.

Pillow Talk

Now it was time for Joy to do her investigation. After getting him erect again and riding him from every imaginable angle, she provided the perfect smoke screen needed for her inquiry. As they laid cuddled up in the sweaty sheets, Joy asked with a soft voice "Soooo, how was night out with the fellas?"

"Not nearly as good as my nights with you my Queen." She hated when he called her that but she was on a mission so she tolerated it

"Of course not..." Joy giggled confidently, "...but I want to make sure that those two womanizers do not corrupt my man's mind...especially that Omar!"

"Actually, Omar has been on his best behavior."

"Meaning?"

"Well Tia's going to give him one last shot but only if he stops being a man whore and make her his one and only...and to tell you the truth, as shocking as it might sound, he's doing better than I would have ever imagined. That Tia must really be special. Who knows, maybe they'll settle down and get married."

"That'll never happen!" Joy exclaimed with a little too much snap in her voice. "I mean, Omar does not seem like the *'settle down'* type."

"I don't know what Tia did to my boy, but trust me; she's the only person in this world that Omar Goodness is powerless against!" Joy tried her best to control her anger.

"Well I guess I'll have to change all of that," Joy thought to herself as she began to drift off into a dream [fantasy?] where Omar was fucking her up the ass so hard that she cried in pure ecstasy.

5 Chap

Latex and Leather

The launch of Goodies Latex and Leather edition that was put together by Becky Nash was phenomenal. The feedback was exceeding all expectations and the, *"rip the runway"* fashion show could only be summed up in one word, "genius!" The models walked the catwalk one at a time wearing different styles of latex and leather lingerie, body suits, and some of the models even displayed whips and floggers that they snapped on the floor as the strutted to the music. What really got the crowed to their feet was when the two Redbone twins, Vick and Veronica walked out together; they were Omar's secret weapons. He had met them at the 40/40 Club a year prior where they had flirted with him and offered to model thongs for Goodies. The Twins worked that catwalk like professionals. Besides, they wanted to impress Omar. The twins had already offered him a once in a lifetime threesome (with identical twin sisters) that piqued his sexual appetite. It seemed that every woman on the planet was throwing herself at Omar now that he had officially taken himself off of the market in his hopes of winning Tia over.

After all the models walked their walk, Omar Goodness and his intern Beck Nash walked the catwalk only to receive a standing ovation. They waved and smiled as they walked hand and hand. Once they made it back behind the curtains, Becky was so excited that she jumped into Omar's arms and wrapped her legs around his waist. Omar was feeling great himself as he spun her 'round and 'round. "You did it!" He shouted with an excited admiration.

"No Omar, *we* did it!" Becky replied. "Now it's time that *we* celebrate!"

2 Hours Later

"No no no... I really can't come inside Becky."

"Don't be silly, what do you like think, that I'll take advantage of my boss? I just need to like, totally show you something before you go home." Omar reluctantly agreed and entered Becky's dark apartment. She walked straight to the back room and closed the door behind herself.

"A LITTLE LIGHT WOULD HELP!" He screamed out as he rubbed his hand on the wall in an attempt to find a light switch.

"Here, let me help." Becky appeared in the darkness, grabbed Omar's hand, and pulled him to the back room. She pushed him down onto her bed. It was obvious that Becky was a few drinks past tipsy and so was Omar. "Wait right here boss...and I'll be right back." She slurred, and then disappeared into her bathroom.

"It's getting late and I really think that I should be going." Omar yelled to the closed door. Instead of responding, Becky came strutting through the door seconds later wearing a see thru latex body suit that had the whole crotch and ass areas cut out. In her hand, she held a leather tasseled whip and on her face, she wore a skintight black leather mask. This had to be the kinkiest thing Omar ever saw in front of him and he was super turned on about it.

"Mr. Omar Goodness, you have brought these new Goodies products into the homes of all the bored to their wits house wives whose biggest fantasy in life is to be submissive to a big strong dominant MAN." Becky walked over to the bed and hands Omar the whip.

"Y…Y…You want me to beat you?" He asked skeptically with excitement in his tone.

Becky bit down on her bottom lip seductively and cat-crawled onto the bed. Omar stood and looked down at her pale but plump little white ass. "No…I do not want you to beat me Omar

Goodness…I want you to punish my ass first with the flogger (the whip) then with your cock."

(*Now this is some freaky shit…Joy ain't got nothing on this chick.*) Omar thought to himself as he raised the flogger up high over his head to strike Becky's plump lil ass.

"Wait!" Becky yelled, as she looked over her shoulder at Omar.

"What's wrong?" He asked, with confusion in his eyes.

"I need you to call me a filthy whore, a dirty slut, and a funky cunt-dog while you punish this ass…okay?"

(*HELL YEAH!*) Omar screamed inside of his head but said to her "okay," in a very simple tone as he came down with the first thrash "YOU FILTHY

WHORE!" (WHACK!). Becky's whole demeanor changed in an instance.

"DON'T BE A LITTLE PUSSY OMAR, PUNISH THIS ASS HARDER!" She screamed in an unrecognizable desperation.

"Oh, you want it harder you dirty slut... (WHACK)...you funky little cunt-dog... (WHACK)...like that bitch!"

"Ummm hmmmmm," Becky moaned as she placed her hand under her dripping wet snatch and began to rub her clit into organism after orgasm while Omar punished her ass and verbally defiled her for the next 30 minutes. Becky pulled a bottle of Platinum lubricant from under her pillow, reached back, and squeezed a niche down her ass crack. "Now fuck this title little ass until you... make me ...cry!" She demanded. Omar looked down and the lube made her asshole look like a shiny little pink balloon knot. Omar dug inside of his pants pocket, retrieved a condom, and then let his pants fall down to his ankles. Becky continued to rub clit as Omar placed the condom on.

"Wait!" She screamed, as Omar grabbed her by her waist to position himself for entry. "Pull my hair back as hard as you can, and don't be a pussy about it, I love pain." Omar yanked her head back with a snatching force then entered Becky's ass like a subway train that had derailed and crashed into the back of other another. Becky howled in pleasure and in pain, which only motivated Omar's thrust to go faster and deeper until he exploded with a body jerking ejaculation.

6 Chap

Guilt Trippin'

The next morning, Omar had finally made it back home. He was completely drained from the all-night fuck fest that Becky Nash put on him. It seemed as if she couldn't get enough and Omar was amazing to her. She lived up to her theory that white girls are like *wild animals* in the bedroom.

Omar's mood was instantly dampened however, when he saw that he had three missed calls from Tia; but it was her text message that made him begin to instantly regret his good time. [Just wanted to congratulate you on the fashion show – you better be behaving yourself.]

Damn, Omar thought to himself as the hot shower water cascaded down on his face and body.

Unexpected Guest

Tia Fields was just getting settled in to her new office at Bailey and Barnes Law Firm when her phone rung, "Attorney at Law, Tia Fields speaking. How can I help you?"

"Listen at you sounding all professional."

Tia recognized the voice instantly, "Brianna Jones…wow this is a surprise. Wait! Don't tell me that you need a lawyer on my first day on the job?"

"Not me, Apple…that girl done got herself in some serious trouble. I called your mom and she gave me this number to reach you at."

(That figures) "Well when can you get down here to my office for a consultation?"

"20 minutes if you are not busy."

"That's perfect. Oh, and Brianna…"

"Yes."

"Bring your checkbook with you."

30 Minutes Later

Bria walked into Tia's office wearing a pair of jeans and sneakers made by Gucci. Her hair was pulled into a long silky ponytail that hung half way down her back. On a dressed down day, Bria was a stunner. Her beauty was natural and her skin was flawless. Tia watched her closely after saying to her "Have a seat please."

Bria looked around the office in admiration. Nodding her head, she said, "This is nice! Look at you, I'm about to cry I am so happy for you." She said with genuine sincerity.

"This little thing...I will be getting a bigger office in no time." Tia bragged with her head tilted to the side. "Okay, now tell me what that crazy friend of yours has done now."

Bria let out an exasperated sigh and relived the whole incident as she told the story "We were in the restaurant and the waitress came over..."

"Good evening, are y'all ready to order?"

"We would like to start with the appetizers." Tia said sweetly. "I would like the fried breaded cheese sticks...and what would you like Apple?"

"Ooooh, I want them apple turn-arounds."

"Do you mean the apple turnovers?" The waitress asked politely. Apple did not like being corrected about her poor grammar and comprehension skills.

"I KNOW WHAT THE HELL THEY CALLED!" She yelled, knowing full well she was lying. "That's just what I call them!" The waitress rolled her eyes at Apple then walked away.

I do not know why I bring this girl with me anywhere knowing that she is going to embarrass me. "Please don't start no mess up in here Apple...I've already had a long day and I just wanna eat and relax." Tia's words go in one ear and other of the other.

"Bitches get they G.E.D. and start acting like they super educated. Did you see that bitch roll her eyes at me? Please…"

"Apple! I'm serious; I'll walk out of here right now! Tia's threat to leave the restaurant instantly calmed Apple down, especially since Tia was treating."

"I'm good but you know how bit--"

"Apple!"

"My bad, but where the appa-teasers at? A bitch is starving." Apple was still looking over her menu when the waitress returned with the appetizers.

"Yes, I will have the Caesar salad, grill the chicken, and hold the croutons." Tia requested considerately.

"Salad!" Apple exclaimed all ghetto like. "Bitches kill me… give me the steak and potatoes…and the chicken and fried shrimp platter."

"And how would you like your steak?" The waitress asked in a courteous tone.

"What?" Apple screwed her face up. "Cooked...how would...Yeah, I want my steak cooked, da fuck you think I want it raw?" Tia had no choice but to further interject before Apple further embarrassed her.

"Well-done please." Again, the waitress rolled her eyes at Apple as she walked off with an attitude that Apple paid no mind to.

"Did I tell you about my new boo?" Apple asked as she stuffed an apple turnover into her mouth.

"I'm not sure. It seems like you have a *'new boo'* every other week." Tia responded sarcastically.

"Don't get cute Miss no boo-at-all."

Twenty minutes later, the waitress returns with their food. Apple snatched a fried shrimp off of the platter before the waitress could even sit the platter on the table. She then looked at the platter and screwed her face up. "Why you let a piece of my girl's salad fall in my food for?"

The waitress could not help but to laugh in Apple's face. "That's not a piece of lettuce...it's actually the garnish."

"Well I didn't order no goddamn garnish and secondly, I'm not paying for it." Tia wanted to run out of the restaurant with her face covered as the waitress laughed even harder now.

"Bitch! What the hell is so damn funny?" Apple screamed as she shot up out of her chair causing a scene.

"I'm laughing at ya ignorant ass...you dumb ghetto ass bit--" The waitress did not finish her insult as Apple charged her with full force and beat the living daylights out of her. When it was all said and done, the waitress suffered a broken nose and she was missing her two front teeth. What made matters worse, was that she told the police that Apple tried to rob her for her tips so now she's sitting in the county jail charged with attempted robbery on top of the assault charge. The judge posted a fifteen thousand dollar bail and Bria had to try and help get her out.

As Bria raked her fingers through her hair, she put on a sad puppy-dog face asked, "So can you get her out?"

"Let me make a few phone calls. I'll see who the Assistant District Attorney on the case is...oh; I still need a retainer's fee."

"Okay. How much?"

"Well I am going to give you the family discount; twenty five hundred dollars for now...but as the case progresses, the fee will enhance."

"That's fine. I'll just stop by your place tonight with the check...the sooner this whole ordeal can be done and dealt with, the better."

7 Chap

Goodies

Omar was in the middle of a very important conference call when Becky Nash entered with a huge smile from ear-to-ear spread across her face. Omar put his finger to his lips gesturing her to be quite. Becky returned his gesture with a gesture of her own. She zipped her lips and threw away the imaginary key. Becky walked around to Omar's desk, stood in front of him, and then dropped down to her knees. Omar panicked; he shook his head while silently saying, *"no!"* but to no avail. Becky pulled out a black leather mask that covered her whole face and head. Omar noticed that the mask only had two holes in it, one for her nose to breathe through, and the other for her mouth. This left Becky totally blindfolded. Becky then unzipped Omar's pants, pulled out his semi-erect penis, and skillfully wrapped her mouth around him. Omar tried to continue with his conference call but fails miserably.

"I...I...I... can draw...uh...draw up... a rough... rough draft." Omar slurred while Becky slurped and gagged as she bobbed her head up and down like woman possessed. The thought of someone walking into the office and catching them in the act, only turned Becky on that much more. She swallowed Omar's ten inches as if she was sucking on her thumb. Omar's eyes rolled to the back of his head as he dropped his phone on the office's carpeted floor. "What the fuck!" He moaned through his clenched teeth.

"Ummmmm," *slurp, slurp* "Um, um, ummmmm" *gag, slurp*. Is all that was heard as Becky continued her oral assault. She could not see a thing (because of the mask), but she could feel Omar's tense build up as he was about to pop. She had one last trick that was sure to blow his mind. She reached down, slipped Omar's expensive Gucci loafers off of his feet, and began thoroughly massaging them, while never losing the rhythm in her neck.

"Beck...oh shit Becky, BECKY!" Omar let out a pleasurable cry as his whole body stiffened. Becky slurped even louder then grabbed Omar's toes to prevent them from curling which left him

powerless over his explosion. "AAAAHHGGHHH"
He screamed as he shot load after load down her
greedy little throat. Becky's throat pleaded for the
cutoff switch but she did not stop until Omar's
whole body went limp. Omar felt as if he was
floating on air when Becky finally released his toes.
Becky stood up, unzipped the back of the black
leather mask, and pulled it off of her head. Streaks
of dried up eyeliner descended down her face from
the tears that all of the gagging had caused. From
the look on Omar's face, Becky knew that this was
his best sexual experience ever. Becky smiled then
said something that blew Omar's mind even more.
"When you are ready to be my God, I will worship
and   please   you   beyond   your   filthiest
imagination…you just say the word my lord." Omar
could only stare at here dumbfounded.

Just What She's Been Missing

As Tia sat behind her laptop reading case law from out of the penal code manual, her mind began to drift into thoughts about Omar Goodness. He hadn't called her in a few days and she began to miss his constant schemes for the cooch. She had already made up her mind that this would be his lucky weekend. She planned on riding his dick into a proposal. The thought of it alone caused her lower parts to heat up.

Tia's craving thoughts were rudely interrupted by the ringing of her doorbell. *Who the hell,* she thought as she walked to the door. After looking through the peephole and seeing Bria, it dawned on her, *the retainers' fee.* Tia opened the door and in stepped Bria, soaking wet from the rain. "Now you know you did not have to come out in all of this rain. I could have waited for the check Brianna."

"Yeah I know, but Apple being in there [being in where?]" drove me crazy." Bria began to cry. Tia rushed over to her and wrapped her arms around her.

"Don't cry everything will be okay." Tia took Bria's pocketbook off of her shoulder and placed it on the coffee table. "Let's get you out of these wet clothes and have a few martinis."

20 minutes later, Bria and Tia sat on the plush carpet reminiscing on old times and trying to figure out what the hell was wrong with Apple's crazy ass. "She's just so quick to fly off the handle whenever somebody looks at her like she's ghetto." Bria

explained causing Tia to look at her as if she was crazy.

"GHETTO?" Tia exclaimed. "That girl is ghetto with a capital G-H-E-T!" They both broke out into laughter and off of shear impulse; Bria stuck her tongue inside of Tia's mouth then sucked her bottom lip into hers. *Ummm* Tia moaned then quickly pulled herself back and said "Whoa! Let me get you your receipt." Tia shot to her feet and dashed inside of her bedroom. Her panties was drenched and her head was spinning. The softness of Bria's lips brought back some unwanted, steamy hot memories. Tia pulled her receipt book out and began to search her nightstand draw for a pen when she felt a pair of arms wrap around her body and felt Bria's soft lips press against her neck. "No

Brianna…we can't…," she pleaded in between her gentle moans.

Bria spun Tia around and began to unbutton her shirt, "Just let me show you how much I miss you." Bria whispered after taking off Tia's bra and letting it drop to the floor.

"Oooooh…yes…" Tia moaned as Bria sucked her left nipple into her warm, wet mouth. Tia grabbed the back of Bria's hair and shifted her head "Don't forget about the other one baby."

"Take these jeans off…please! I want that pussy so bad. Hurry please!" Bria begged and Tia obliged, stripping down until she was fully nude and Bria did the same.

Tia backpedaled to the bed, laid down, and cocked her legs back as far as they could go, which left her kneecaps pressed against her earlobes. "Its jumping baby…you got this pussy jumping…come get it NOW!" Tia screamed in horny ecstasy. Bria dove in tongue first. It had been so long since the last time she indulged in Tia's nectar, that she almost forgot how blissful she tasted.

"Ummmmm, slurp…you taste so fucking good. Umm hmm sluuuurp."

"Damn baby, I feel it coming already…don't stop, don't stop, yeeeeesss, right there…please don't stop!" Tia looked down at Bria's lips wrapped around her clit and that pretty much sealed the deal as she began to cum violently. "Eeeewwwwllll!" She let out a scream that did not sound like it came from a human as her body shook uncontrollably like a major earthquake. *"Grrrrhh…grrrrhhh…grrrrrrr."*

Bria took this as a sign to go even harder, "Unnnnnnn…unnn…un…" She flicked her tongue in circles all around Tia's sensitive clit, which caused shock waves to shoot through Tia's body. "Unnnnn...un..." She moaned. Tia felt herself quickly building back up and this point, Bria had her speaking on tongues.

"Bbbb...bae...babe...baby...yeahes...I'm...bbb b...bout...to...sq...sq...squirt!" And just like that, her pussy exploded as if someone had just shook a bottle of Pepsi up and then opened the top. It was a struggle for Tia to pull away from Bria's death clutches."

"I'll be right back, don't move." Bria demanded. It wasn't as if Tia had the strength to move anyway. Bria walked out of the room, dug into her pocketbook and pulled out a 9-inch rubber strap-on and a bottle of lubricant. After strapping it on, she walked back into the bedroom with a full *erection.* Tia gasped when she saw it.

"Oh my god Brianna! Since when--"

"Never, but I want to try it with you okay?" Bria explained as she crawled into the bed.

"I don't know...I...ooooh..." being caught off guard as Bria suddenly rubbed the lube onto her hot twat.

"Turn that ass around." Bria said in a serious no nonsense manner. Tia obliged and positioned herself doggy-style (WHAP!) Bria smacked her on the ass causing it to jiggle; she then slid inside of her slowly. If only Bria could feel Tia's tightness as she began to slide in and out.

"Ooh...ooh...ooooooh...Brianna that feels so fucking good!"

"Want me to go deeper baby?"

"Yes, please."

"Faster too?"

"Oh yes!"

"Harder too baby?" Bria asked seductively as she began to thrust faster, harder and deeper.

"Slap my ass...slap it (Whack!) Bria did as she was told. "Now pull...my...hair." Tia further instructed between moans. When she felt her hair being pulled back, she began to throw her ass back viscously.

"That's right, fuck me back." (Whack!) Bria smacked her ass even harder. She couldn't believe how turned on Tia was.

"Oh shit...I'm about...to cum all over...this dick baby."

"Come on...cum for me baby (WHACK!) Cum for me!" (WHACK!)

"Oh shit...here it cum baby....here it... cuuuuuummmms..."

"Bria began to fuck her harder "Scream my name...whose pussy is this Tia!"

"Oh my god I'm CUMMMMING!"

"Say my name!"

Tia's brain turned into noodles as her body shivered, so when Bria demanded that she say her name while she was cumming, Tia slipped and screamed "OMAR!" Everything went quiet like when the D.J. cuts the music off and Bria screamed with an attitude!

"WHAT THE FUCK!"

8 Chap

Trouble Maker

O mar Goodness sat behind his desk at his Goodies warehouse thinking about the contract that Becky Nash had them sign three days ago, where they both agreed that Omar would be her "God." Omar heard of people signing contracts when dealing with slaves but he had never heard of anything remotely close to what Becky Nash agreed to. It was the first three lines of the contract that was stuck in his mind, day in and day out.

NUMBER ONE: I will worship you and only you my Lord.

NUMBER TWO: I will obey any and every sexual demand that you desire my Lord.

NUMBER THREE: My mind, Body and Soul belongs to you my Lord.

Omar's thoughts were interrupted by a commotion outside of his office. Before he could get up to see what was going on, his door was pushed open with enough force to almost break the glass. He was shocked but not surprised as it was Joy who had stormed into his office. He had already washed his hands with her for months now but according to her, that dick was hers for L.I.F.E. "Why the hell have you been avoiding me Omar?" She screamed in a sexually frustrated tone. Omar stood up, walked past Joy, and locked his office door, then, he sat back down behind his desk.

"Listen Joy, I…"

"No you listen! I want some dick!" Joy began to undress which caused Omar to jump up.

"Joy! Cut it out, we are not having sex in my office! I run a respectable business around and I…" (WHACK!) Joy smacked the words out of Omar's mouth.

"FUCK ME NOW OMAR!" She went to swing again but Omar caught her hand mid swing. He twisted her arm behind her back then bent her over the desk.

"Do not make me call the police on you Joy…go home!" Omar said sternly as he released her. Joy began to cry.

"Please Omar...I...I really need it so...bad..." She sobbed and sniffles in between her words.

"I'm sorry Joy, but I'm swamped with work and..."

"BULLSHIT OMAR! That bitch Tia has you twisted around her little finger but I will kill her before I let her take that dick away from me. I will kill her dead!" The crazed look in Joy's eyes revealed to Omar exactly how serious she was and it definitely startled him to a degree.

"Joy, listen to me; you really need to get some help. You cannot threaten to take someone's life because you can't have sex with me anymore. There are millions of guys that will love to give it to you every way that you desire."

"Save it Omar. Either be at my house Friday night or make arrangements for her funeral." Joy said calmly then walked out of the office leaving Omar sitting there dumbfounded.

Criminal Court

Tia Fields walked into the courtroom wearing a navy blue pinstriped pantsuit. Her six inch heals clicked loudly as she walked through the aisle. Tia noticed Bria and gave her a professional head nod. Bria rolled her eyes then turned her head dismissingly. She was still beyond pissed at Tia for calling out Omar's name three nights ago.

Minutes later, Apple's case was being called and out she came wearing an orange prison jumpsuit with her hair cornbraided down her back. "You Honor, my client is willing to plead out to a misdemeanor in exchange for 150 hours of community service and undergo a sixth month anger management program if the court deems it proper."

A half hour later, Tia, Bria, and Apple were driving away from the court building in Tia's car. Apple hadn't shut her mouth yet. "Yeah, I had shit on lock in there. Bitches was sweating me, fiending to lick this pus…"

"Apple!" Bria exclaimed, "Nobody wants to hear about your big house adventure. I was out here worried to death!"

"Didn't I tell you that I could handle myself? I grew up with six brothers and I use to beat the hell out of four of them!"

"Bria, why haven't you returned any of my calls?" Tia asked as she made the left turn into Apple's block. Bria ignored her as if she hadn't heard her at all.

"Ooooh, what I miss?" Apple asked, picking up the vibe instantly, "Let me find out...I have been doing hard time and y'all being doing each other." Neither Bria nor Tia responded so Apple pressed even harder, "So y'all made up and broke up again? That was fast; what did you do this time Bria?"

"Me! Why did it have to be me?"

"Because it's always you, bitch, "Apple said with a smirk."

"Well, not this time Miss Know-It-All," Bria replied matter of factly.

9 Chap

Friday Night

Omar dressed casually for his date with Tia. Joy's threat to harm Tia lingered in the back of his mind.

He had told Tia that he was coming to pick her up. Omar opened his door to find a smiling Becky at his doorstep. *"What the hell?"* he thought to himself. "Ugh, what are you doing here, Becky?" Omar asked with a confused look on his face.

"Sorry, Mr. Goodness, but this like totally could not wait. Goodies Latex and Leather line has just got even kinkier and ---"

"I'm sorry Becky, but this will have to wait until tomorrow. I'm on my way to ---"

"Don't be silly. This will only take a minute; if that?" Becky walked past Omar and into his home. Neither of them knowing that Joy sat across the street recording their interaction on her Smart phone. Her blood was boiling. Just the thought of Omar curving her for a white girl had her hands shaking.

"So what's so important Becky?"

Becky pulled out what looked to be a shiny white mouthpiece. She handed it to Omar with a smile on her face. Omar observed that the object was definitely some sort of mouthpiece made out of latex. "What in the world is this?" he asked.

"It's called Gummy Gum," Becky said as he placed the object into her mouth. "It gives the rough surface of teeth a smooth gummy feeling and it gets very slippery when wet. So there will be no more scraping of the cock, but there's only one problem, Mr. Goodness."

"And that would be?"

"It hasn't been tested as of yet." Becky dropped to her knees and reached for Omar's zipper.

"WHOA... Becky! I can't! I'm late for a very important ---"

"Yeah, yeah, I know, but this is business boss," Becky said cutting him off. Becky's aggressive seduction was too powerful to resist. She freed Omar's hard-on and inserted him into her mouth.

The term "slippery when wet," was an understatement when it came to describing the Gummy Gum!"

"OH SHIT!" Omar growled. The sensation was unexplainable and the squishing sound that the wet latex made enhanced the pleasure by ten.

"Ummmm... Umm...Hmmm," Becky moaned as she picked up her speed. It took a total of forty-two seconds for Omar to shoot rockets of cum to the back of her throat. Becky snatched him from her mouth and took the last two squirts to the face. Becky inserted him back into her mouth and began to softly chew down on his sensitive and tender head. The soft texture of the Gummy Gum caused Omar to let out a not so masculine squeal. He tried pushing Becky's head back, but she would not release him from her mouth.

"I...I...I...can't...take...it! Please stop," Becky shook her head no and continued to chew.

Meanwhile

Joy had exited her car as soon as Omar and Becky entered his home. She crept around to an open window that had the curtains already pulled back and watched as Becky placed the shiny object into her mouth, drop to her knees, and commence to suck the hell out of Omar's dick. Joy pulled her phone out and recorded it all with one hand while she placed her other hand down in her pants and rubbed her clit with the speed of someone who was possessed. The sight of Omar's dick disappearing down in Becky's throat made her cum almost as quickly as Becky made Omar cum.

The Next Morning

Omar awoke to an empty house. Becky literally sucked him to sleep. Never in his life did he bust three nuts back-to-back from getting head until last night. Omar reached for his phone and read his first text message. It was from Tia.

I can't believe that you stood me up Omar. Oh well... Your loss!

The next text was from Becky. She must have sent it after she left his home.

Thank you for blessing me with your almighty cock, my Lord. I worship no God, but thee.

The last text that he read was from Joy.

I got your selfish ass this time Omar! Be at my house tomorrow afternoon, or else I'll send this video to Tia.

Omar played the video of Becky sucking is cock and his mouth fell wide the hell open. He jumped up, dressed, and headed to Joys' house.

Joyous

The door was unlocked as usual. Omar barged in and headed straight up the stairs to find Joy's bedroom door locked.

"JOY, OPEN THIS GODDAMN DOOR!" Omar screamed as he banged on the door.

Joy laid back on her bed wearing a lace panty and bra set made by Goodies with a twelve-inch dildo half way down her throat. She pulled it from her mouth with a loud wet "PLOP" and yelled at the door, "KICK IT THE HELL OPEN!"

"OPEN THE DOOR, JOY!"

"CAN THAT WHITE BITCH, SUCK IT BETTER THAN ME, OMAR?"

BOOM!

Omar kicked the door in and Joy's panties became drenched with her juices. Omar raced over to the bed, snatched the dildo out of Joy's mouth, and roughly flipped her over onto her stomach.

"THAT'S RIGHT! NO MERCY ON THIS PUSSY! YOU BETTER SMASH IT IN OR I'M TELLING TIA!"

"BITCH, YOU'RE NOT TELLING TIA ANY FUCKING THING!" Omar screamed using both hands as he began to rip the lace panties off of Joy's ass. Joy bit down on her bottom lip and surprised when Omar tried to wrap the panties around her throat with only a little room left for her to breath.

Next, Omar slid her ponytail through the panties pulling Joy's head back while choking her at the same time. Joy go on her hands and knees anticipating Omar to enter her from behind. Instead, he pulled her ponytail tight causing her to choke and gag a little. Then he picked up the twelve-inch dildo and began to beat her all over her ass with it. *WHACK!*

Joy cried out in pure pleasure and pain exactly how Becky Nash did when she made him beat her over the ass with the leather whip. *WHACK!*

"YES OMAR, YESSSS!" *WHACK!*

"I won't tell... I swear..." *WHACK!*

"OH MY GOD, OMAR... YOU GONNA MAKE ME... CUM!" *WHACK! WHACK! WHACK!*

"I'M CUM... I'M CUUUMMMMING!"

Omar tossed the dildo to the floor, pulled his pants down to his knees, and entered Joy's hot soaking wet pussy with a force to be reckon with. As much as he hated Joy at that very moment, there was no way of denying that her cooch was fire.

He pounded and pounded until he couldn't hold back any longer. "AAARRRGGH!" he screamed as he pulled out almost an extra pump too late, shooting warm cum all over the outside of Joy's pussy. Omar fell to the side in slow motion. He laid there cursing himself out for damn near slipping up. Just the thought of an accidental pregnancy with Joy was enough to scare him and his dick half to death.

Joy laid there smiling to herself knowing that not only did she have the footage of him and the white girl, now she had footage of him and herself thanks to Bria who convinced her to buy the Nanny

Cam that sat discreetly on the top of her dresser. Omar Goodness was about to truly become her sex slave whether he liked it or not.

"Don't you go to sleep back there. I'm going to take a quick shower and then you are going to eat this pussy until I see stars," Joy said in a demanding no-nonsense manner. "Do you understand me?"

"Yes," Omar mumbled.

"Yes Master!" Joy ordered.

"Excuse me?"

"Say, yes Master!"

Omar hesitated, questioning if Tia was worth him going through all of this. Then without a second thought, he replied.

"Yes---" He let out a loud sigh. "Yes... Master!"

10 Chap

Mrs. Lee's Nail Salon

"Well, well, well... Looky who the cat dragged in," Mrs. Lee said with her face twisted into a fake frown.

"Stop playing Mrs. Lee. You know you miss me," Millie replied with a huge cheesy smile on her face. Millie had left about a year ago to go to Atlanta to pursue her acting career which did not go well, and now she was back home looking thicker than a snicker; in all the right places. The southern cooking, mixed with a strict exercise regimen got her a lot of offers to be in some of the top selling ATL hip hop artist's booty shaking videos, but she always politely declined.

Mrs. Lee looked at Millie's fingernails and joked, "What, you work as construction lady worker?"

"Ha… Ha… Ha… Just hook me up for old time sake. Plus you know you have to fill me in on all the latest gossip."

"Me? Me know gossip? Well, I did hear things!" Mrs. Lee being the Chinese Queen of gossip wasted no time spilling the beans. "Well, friend come Friday and gets nails done all jazzy for date with the man y'all fight over."

Millie's mouth dropped open. "Omar Goodness? Are you sure, Mrs. Lee?"

"Umm... Hmm... Friend say everybody deserves second chance."

Hearing this shocking news gave Millie an instant attitude. Oh, she was definitely feeling some type of way. *"Now, I'll be wrong if I get back on my bullshit,"* Millie thought to herself.

The Cold Shoulder

"Mrs. Fields, there is an Omar Goodness in the waiting area. Should I send him in?" the firm's secretary informed Tia.

"No, let Mr. Goodness know that I'm extremely busy and he will have to schedule another appointment," Tia said without raising her head from the omnibus motion that she was preparing for one of her clients. Tia could feel the secretary's presence still standing over her. She raised her head as to say, *"Anything else?"*

The secretary leaned her head to the side, put on a puppy-dog face, and said, "He has flowers." Her face said, *"And he's a millionaire."*

Tia gave the secretary a stern, "get the hell out of my office," look causing her to back out in a surrender. Five minutes later, she could hear the secretary saying, "Sir! You cannot go back there! I---." The door swung open and there stood Omar Goodness.

"Omar!" Tia exclaimed.

"I'm sorry baby. I just need one minute."

"Baby?" Tia asked in surprise and then turned to her secretary. "Sarah, give me thirty seconds."

Tia turned to Omar, "Are you crazy? You could get me fired."

"I'll get you, your own firm!"

"Twenty seconds left," Tia said.

"Okay, okay... Look, I have no excuse. I put business before you and it will never happen again. Just tell me how I can make it up to you! Please!" Omar begged.

"Well, I'm not sure as of yet. If and I really do mean "IF" I think of something, I'll let you know." With the quickness of a cat, Omar moved in, picked Tia up, and sat her down on the edge of her desk. "What the hell are you doing?" Tia whispered in shock.

"Showing you how sorry I am." Omar pushed her legs apart, reached his hands under her skirt, and before she could protest, he was ripping her panties off forcefully. Tia wanted to stop him, but she was turned on by his take-charge aggressiveness. Omar rolled her skirt up to her waist, dropped to his knees, and orally assaulted her hot spot.

Tia bit down on the palm of her hand to try and prevent herself from moaning loudly, but it only muffled her cry of pleasure. Whatever Omar was doing down there, she was afraid that if she looked down, she would pass the hell out again.

"Omar, O… Mar…," she whispered.

"Hmmm?" *SLURP! SLURP! SLURP!*

"You… better… be… at my house… ummm… tonight!"

SLUUUURRRRRP! SLURP! SLURP!

"Right there! Don't stop! I'm about to… Bout to…" Just as Tia was about to fill Omar's mouth with her hot thick juices, there was three loud knocks at the door, instantly killing her orgasm.

KNOCK! KNOCK! KNOCK!

"Mrs. Fields, you have a client who wishes to see you," the secretary said through the closed door. Tia pushed Omar from between her legs, wiped her juices off of his face, and then told him sternly, "If you are not at my house by ten, forget you ever knew me!"

Surprise!

Later that night, Omar parked his car outside of Tia's home. He made sure that he was thirty minutes early because there was no way he was going to miss his opportunity to blow Tia's back out. The cat and mouse game ended tonight. Omar stepped out of his car, popped his collar, and as he went to turn, he came mouth to mouth with the softest lips ever. He felt himself backpedaling and being pressed against his car. A set of hands reached down and squeezed his dick through his think slacks. Omar wiggled out of the tight spot after being seductively bit on his neck.

"What the---"

"Did you miss me?" Millie asked and then did a full spin giving Omar an up and close look at her newfound curves that the formfitting dress she was wearing complimented in every way possible.

"M...Millie?" he stuttered with his eyes glued to her figure.

"Long time no see, no feel, no taste," she said licking her lips and then she blew a kiss at him.

"Wow! You look so, so, so good!"

"And it will forever be yours," Millie said turning and giving Omar her back, lifting up her skirt, and exposing her O.M.G. tattoo and her hot pink thong by Goodies. Instead of pulling her skirt back down, Millie walked back to her car with her whole ass out. It was damn near double the size it was about a year ago, and Omar could not take his eyes off of it as it bounced up and down with every step she took. Millie opened her car door and looked over her shoulder.

"My number is still the same." To add emphasis, Millie smacked her right cheek causing it to jiggle. Omar almost ran after her, but he composed himself knowing that there was no pussy like new pussy.

Tia's

Omar rang the doorbell once and the door was immediately opened by Tia. She wore a black silk nighty by Goodies with a pair of six-inch pumps on her feet. "Damn baby! You looking like steak and I'm starving," Omar said licking his lips. Tia grabbed him by the shirt and yanked him into the house. She was on fire.

It had been so long since the last time she had a hard dick pounding into her hot box that she almost tripped over her feet dragging Omar to her bedroom. She pushed him down on the bed, walked over to her nightstand, picked up a lighter, and then walked around her room lighting candle after candle. There were fifteen in total. By the time she finished, Omar had already stripped down naked.

Tia turned on her new R-Kelly album and did a sexy striptease in front of Omar and then she climbed on top of him in a straddling position.

"I must warn you, Omar. This pussy stays wetter than the ocean and it's three years tight, so try to hold on as long as…" Tia slid down on his dick, "possible!"

"Damn Tia," Omar whispered in pleasure as Tia began a slow, but intense grind.

"Ummmmmm," Tia said as she bent down and passionately kissed Omar as she continued to grind slowly. "Yeeeeessss Omar! Is this pussy wet enough for you?"

"Yes baby…It's soaking wet, baby!"

"Can I go faster?"

"Yes!"

Tia picked up her speed just enough to match the rhythm of the R-Kelly song. "Omar?"

"Yes baby."

"Can…I cum…all…over this…dick?"

"Come on, cum for me…cum for me…"

"Okay! Okay! Here I, here I...cum! I'm cum...cum...I'M CUMMMMMIN! AHHHHHH! O! I'm cum...cum...I'M CUMMMMMIN! AHHHHHH! OOOOOOH!" Tia's body began to shiver as her pussy exploded warm cum down Omar's shaft. "Oh, do you feel it Omar? Do you feel it?" she cried out in ecstasy.

"Yes baby! I feel you! I...I...I....love you!" As soon as the words left Omar's mouth, he exploded inside of Tia's gushing cooch. His brain told him to pull out, but her pussy told his mind to shut the hell up.

Omar and Tia made passionate love for the remainder of the night. They had told each other, I love you at least fifteen times apiece before the sun came up. Sex with Tia felt so clean, so normal, and so damn good that Omar truly felt as though he had

just lost his virginity on a whole different level.

11 Chap

Cold Hearted

"**B**aby, I don't understand. I thought everything was going well. Was it something I did? Can I please come inside? Maybe we can figure this out together."

"Listen Kinard, I have to be brutally honest with you. You are a sweet guy, but you are not capable of fucking me half to death so it's over!" Joy slammed the door in Kinard's face. Now that she had Omar as her sex slave, there was no more use for Kinard's righteous bullshit.

Jay laid back on her bed after removing her shirt and bra. She reached inside of her nightstand and pulled out a set of silver nipple clamps that were attached to a small chain. Her hands began to shake as she positioned them and then clamped them onto her erect nipples. Joy yelped in pain and then pressed play on the TV. She and Omar's sex tape appeared on the screen.

Watching Omar beat her pussy up as if an animal turned her into a ball of fire. Joy began to yank on the chain. The pain made her eyes water and her pussy drip. She started to pick up the phone to call Omar and demand him to come over to her house, but quickly decided against it. What she had in store for him in a few days would be epic.

Joy was just about to rub her clit into an orgasm when she was interrupted by the ringing of her doorbell. Out of pure frustration, she jumped out of her bed and stormed to her door. She looked through the peephole and saw Brianna standing there. *"What the heck does she want?"* she thought to herself as she snatched the door wide open. It wasn't until Brianna's mouth fell wide open that Joy realized that she was buck-naked with nipple clamps hanging from her breast.

"Girl, why are you naked?" Bria asked as she quickly stepped inside and closed the door behind herself. "Your neighbors would be traumatized!"

"Bria, I'm not sure if you noticed, but ummm, I'm kind of in the middle of something."

"I'm sorry. I just needed someone to talk to. Can you believe Tia screamed Omar's name when we were having sex?"

Joy was sexually frustrated and it showed when she spoke. "Listen Bria, I'm sorry to inform you, but there's no way in the world you could handle Tia the way Omar can. That man is a Vagina Connoisseur and to make matters worse, his tongue is freaking computerized! Trust me, I know! Now if that will be all, I would like to---" Joy's words were pushed back into her mouth by Bria's tongue.

When Bria stopped for air, she demanded, "Well I guess you will be the official judge. This tongue never made a bitch faint, but it did make a bitch leave her husband, two kids, house, and dog." Bria ducked her head and grabbed the chain that was hanging from Joy's nipples with her teeth. The pain that shot through Joy's body caused her to stand on her tippy toes. She bit down on her bottom lip seductively and whispered, "Bri...Bria, I'm...not...into...women."

Bria leaned down and stuck her finger inside of Joy's pussy. "Oh really? Then why are you so wet?" she asked as she twirled her fingers inside of Joy and tugged on the chain a little harder.

"Ooooooh fuck! That hurt sooooo good! Ummmm yes!" Joy moaned in painful pleasure. "Don't stop Bria!"

Bria did not want to lose control of the situation so she pulled her fingers out of Joy real slow and then placed them in her mouth.

"Ummmmm... You taste like an Almond Joy." Bria made sure she licked Joy's juices completely off of her fingers and then she grabbed the chain again and pulled Joy towards the bedroom. "Let's go! Let me show you that it's levels to this thing,"

Bria said seductively. Bria pushed Joy's bedroom door open with her free hand and they both walked in.

"WHAT THE FUCK?" she screamed as soon as she entered and saw Omar fucking the living hell out of Joy on the flat screen. "You got him on the Nanny Cam and did not tell me, Joy?" she screamed in frustration.

"Choke me harder...motherfucker...HARDER!" Joy screamed at Omar on the screen.

Joy tried to walk over to the flat screen to turn it off, but Bria yanked the chain a little harder than she intended to cause Joy to gasp. Bria started to apologize, but the look of pleasure on Joy's face spoke in volume. *"This bitch like pain,"* Bria thought yanking the chain downward bringing Joy to her knees.

"Bitch, you about to learn to do what the fuck I say! Now get ya ass up and get doggy style on the fucking bed...NOW!" Bria screamed. She wasn't in character, she was really pissed that Joy had withheld the leverage that she so needed to keep Omar away from Tia.

Joy did as she was told. Bria crawled on the bed and squatted over her. She roughly pushed her legs apart and reached under her body until she felt the chain and then she yanked it even harder this time causing Joy's whole body to shake uncontrollably. "Now I want you to count to three, real slow," Bria said aggressively and without any hesitation, Joy obliged. She just loved to be dominated.

"One...Two...Three." Then Joy screamed as Bria pulled the chain extra hard and rammed her whole tongue inside of Joy's tight little asshole.

Bria kept her eyes trained on the flat screen. One thing she did have to admit was that Omar Goodness was a beast in the sheets. The more Bria watched, the more turned on she got. She tried to convince herself that it was Joy's screams that had her pussy dripping, but deep down inside she knew that it was Omar's aggression that was making her pussy jump.

It actually pissed her off so she took it out on Joy. WHACK! She smacked Joy's ass so hard that Joy had to bite down on the pillow to keep from screaming.

"OMAR! OMAR! OOOOOMAR!"

"What bitch? What?" he screamed as he continued to pound Joy's back out on the screen.

"I'M BOUT TO FUCKNG SQUIRT!"

Bria watched as Omar quickly pulled his huge dick out of Joy and then bent her legs all the way back to her shoulders.

"TELL ME! TELL ME BITCH!" Omar barked as Joy rubbed her clit furiously. "TELL ME!"

"I…I LOVE THAT DICK!" Joy screamed and then she squirted damn near a quart of her juices all over Omar's chest and six-pack.

Bria's body began to quiver as she watched Omar grab Joy by the hair and make her lick her juices off of his chest. Not realizing how hard she was pulling the chain and tonguing Joys' ass, Joy began to cum all over Bria's neck. "AAAAAHHHHHGGH!" The only thing on Bria's mind was getting the footage to hold against Omar and she knew exactly how to do it.

"Now turn this pussy over bitch so I can turn your freak ass the fuck out!" Joy did exactly what she was told to do. Bria crawled up her body and grabbed her tightly by the throat. Joy could barely breathe as she stared up at Bria. "Now welcome to my world," Bria said and then sat her hot pussy on Joy's mouth before Joy could protest. Bria humped her face so fast that she felt her orgasm coming on quickly. "Open your mouth," she screamed, but Joy shook her head no. Bria squeezed her throat harder and then reached back with her free hand and pulled the chain so hard that the right clamp came off. Joy's toes began to curl.

"Bitch, I said open your fucking mouth!" This time Joy did as she was told. Bria's eyes rolled to the back of her head as she bit down on her bottom lip. She let out the loudest screeching sex cry that

Joy had ever heard and then she gushed a puddle into Joy's mouth. At first, Joy was disgusted by it, but her inner freak caused her to swallow every drop. Joy shocked her damn self when she wanted more and began to suck Brianna's pussy. "That's right! Eat that pussy Joy! Just like that bitch, you like it, don't you?"

Joy nodded her head yes, stuck her thumb in Bria's ass, and began to suck on Bria's clit. "Oh yeah, I'm definitely going to get that tape," Bria thought as she looked down at Joy's soaking wet mouth, cheeks, and chin.

12 Chap

Look What the Wind Blew

In

Tia sat at her desk looking over her caseload. She was starting to make a name for herself as the new and upcoming pit-bull in a skirt defense attorney. Her first trial was set to start in a few weeks. Her client was accused of stabbing a taxicab driver to death in the middle of a robbery. Her client pleaded not guilty, claiming that the cabbie was a close friend of his and that the altercation started over twenty dollars' worth of crack that they were supposed to share. Her client claimed that the cabbie attacked him and he only acted in self-defense when he felt that his life was in danger.

Tia raked her fingers through her hair as her mind drifted off to the way Omar made sweet love to her. *"I could most definitely get used to that,"* she thought to herself not even realizing the Kool-Aid smile that was spreading across her face. Her thoughts were interrupted by the ringing of her office phone.

"Attorney at Law, Tia Fields, how may I help you," she stated professionally.

"BITCH, STAY AWAY FROM MY MAN! YOU'VE BEEN WARNED!"

CLICK!

The phone went dead in Tia's ear causing her to look at the receiver with a confused look on her face. Tia hung up the phone, grabbed her pocketbook, and left the office with nothing but Omar Goodness on her mind, well him and lunch. She was hungry as hell and headed to her favorite restaurant.

Tia was halfway through her meal when she literally lost her appetite. She started to get up and leave, but she was a second too late. Millie invaded her space wearing the phoniest smile.

"Hey girl! Long time no see," Millie exclaimed only to receive a cold stare from Tia, which was no surprise to Millie. "Damn girl! I know you are not still mad at me. I thought we promised each other when we were kids to never let a man come in between us."

Tia rolled her eyes with a serious head swirl. "Millie, this is not about Omar! It's about your trifling dick-chasing ass! How could you do that to me?" Tia's voice cracked, but Millie was soulless on the inside.

"Look, I understand the pain I've caused, but if you can forgive Omar, then I just can't get why you can't forgive me... We've been friends for way too long."

"And who said that I forgave Omar?"

Millie smiled at her once upon a time friend and then decided to be unapologetically honest. "Who could be mad at a tongue and dick game like Omar's for too long?"

Tia felt a flash of hot rage surge through her body. She stood to leave, but decided to give Millie something to think about. "Well, I hope you enjoyed it because I'm pretty sure you'll never get it again."

Millie bust out laughing. "If that's your way of "ASKING" me to stay away from your man, then you could at least say please. But look, you don't have to worry about me. Just keep a short leash on your "MAN" because he will come sniffing around. He might love you, but he most definitely love this pussy!" Millie spun around and left the restaurant as quick as she came, leaving Tia standing there fuming.

Goodies

Omar sat behind his desk physically drained from the all-nighter he had with Tia a day and a half ago. He tried to focus on the monthly spreadsheets, but his eyes began to get heavy as he yawned for the millionth time. Just as Omar began to drift off, Becky Nash entered his office. "Good afternoon, My Lord. Is there anything I can do for you, or is there anything you would like to do to me?" Omar was too out of it to entertain the whole "Sex God" character so he tried to wave her off politely.

"No, I pretty much have everything--," Omar yawned. "Under control." Becky walked behind Omar's chair and began to massage his shoulders and neck. He started to protest, but her hands felt better than a thousand milligrams of muscle relaxers.

"You just relax My Lord; rest yourself."

Omar drifted off into a deep sleep within seconds. Becky's inner freak screamed inside of her head, *"LIKE WHAT ARE YOU WAITING FOR? SUCK HIS COCK!"* Becky shook the thought off just as Omar's cellphone sounded off indicating that he had received a text message. She started to ignore it, but curiosity got the best of her. Becky picked up the phone and read the message.

Tia 12:16p.m.

When were u going 2 tell me that your little slut Millie was back in town. I'm not going thru this again. We need 2 talk. My place @ 8.

Becky quickly texted her back.

Okay, 8 it is.

Then she deleted both of the messages from Omar's phone. Two minutes later, Omar received another text.

Joy 12:18p.m.

Bring that dick to me tonight and make sure it's rock hard and pulsating when you get here.

Becky glanced over at the snoring Omar Goodness and then responded to Joy's text.

Maybe another time.

Before Becky could delete the messages, Joy was already responding.

Joy 12:20p.m.

Omar, do not make me show Tia what you've been up to. I'm sure it'll break her heart... again! LOL BRING ME MY DICK... Be a good slave.

Becky could not believe what she was reading. Omar Goodness was being blackmailed for sex, and not only that, whoever Tia was, it was clear that she and Omar were in a supposed to be committed relationship. Becky erased the messages and then sat Omar's phone back on his desk. She was in deep thought when Omar's phone sounded off again. She picked it up in a hurry, only to find that someone had sent Omar a picture of her ass that had O.M.G. tattooed across the right cheek with the following message.

Millie 12:25p.m.

This will always be your ass!

Becky put one and one together quickly. Millie was the one that Tia had texted Omar about a little while ago. The way Becky saw it was Millie and Joy were not a threat. They were Omar's toys, but Tia would surely come in between her and her sex God, so she did the only logical thing that came to her mind. Becky dropped to her knees in between Omar's legs, pulled his cock out, and slowly sucked him to an erection without awakening him. Next Becky grabbed Omar's phone, snapped a picture of his cock, and then sent it to Millie with the following text message.

And this dick will always be yours.

She placed Omar's cock back in his pants, erased all of the text messages from his phone, and then left him sleep in his office. When she walked out of his office, she thought to herself, *"Tia totally has to go!"*

2 Hours Later

Omar was awakened by the weirdest thing ever. Well not exactly, but he was definitely caught off guard. Becky had both of his balls in her mouth tickling them with her tongue.

"B...B...Becky...Stop...It!" Omar gently pushed her back by her shoulders causing her to PLOP his balls out of her mouth. She wiped the saliva off of her chin with the back of her hand.

"Just pleasing your Holy Scrotum, My Lord."

"Becky, please. The whole Sex God thing is---"

"IS WHAT?" Becky screamed letting her sex craved frustration show. "If you want me to behave like your slave, you're going to have to beat this fucking cunt into goddamn submission! You're going to have to ram that cock in this pick little asshole, balls deep, OMAR!"

20 Minutes Later

Omar walked through the front door of his lavish home. Becky followed close behind him with her head to the ground in full submissive mode.

Omar had a surge of energy run through his body that he didn't know existed. "Drop to your knees and crawl through the house of God, my disobedient child."

"Yes, My Lord," she replied and did what she was told. Becky crawled all the way to Omar's bedroom, which was up a flight of stairs.

"Get on top of the bed, strip naked, and get positioned for your lashing."

"Yes, My Lord," Becky said excitedly. Within seconds, she was nude with her face down in a pillow and her ass in the air. Omar removed his belt, raised it above his head, and then came down on Becky's ass with a force to be reckoned with.

"AHHHHRRRRRG!" Becky screamed. Her scream shrieked, but she managed to look over her shoulder and tell Omar, "HARDER!" She bit down on the pillow awaiting the next strike thinking to herself, *"Sorry Tia and sorry Joy because Omar's not coming over tonight."*

13 Chap

All Hell

"Did you not get my text last night?" Tia asked with an obvious attitude.

"Yeah, but I---"

"Save it Omar! You probably was out chasing after that nasty hoe!"

"Tia, I do not have the slightest idea who or what you're talking about."

"I'm talking about Millie. She approached me on my lunch break talking about it's only a matter of time before you come running back to her."

Omar chuckled. "Haven't we not learned to take a grain of salt with everything that comes out of that girl's mouth?" Omar's phone rang, interrupting Tia's comeback. Omar looked at Joy's name on the caller ID, quickly sent her to voicemail, and then tucked his phone away.

"Who was that?"

"Excuse me? Tia, what's gotten into you lately? You're becoming someone else. This is not you."

Tia raked her fingers through her hair and dropped her head, "I'm sorry. I just don't want to lose you to her again... I ---"

"Tia," Omar interjected. "When it comes to my heart, trust me, it's all yours!"

"What about that dick? How many bitches do I have to share that with?" Omar's phone rang again, but this time it was a threatening text from Joy.

Joy 4:19p.m.

Don't say I didn't warn you. Now I'll show you not to fuck with me, Omar Goodness.

Omar's heart skipped a beat not knowing what Joy's crazy ass would do. With the speed of God, he texted her back.

DON'T! I'm on my way!

Omar stood up, grabbed his jacket, kissed Tia on the cheek, and said, "I have to go." He ran out of Tia's apartment so fast that he didn't notice the hurt and disgusted look that was plastered across her face.

Joy's

"No, I am not going to let you handcuff me to the bed, Joy," Omar barked in a weak attempt to try and put his foot down once and for all as he stood there in the nude.

"Okay well, this is not fun! You can leave." Joy stared Omar down almost daring him to leave her house. Omar read through her antics instantly.

"Okay, but you better un-cuff me when we're done or I'll rip your whole bedpost off; understand?"

"Just lay down and stop being a wuss!" Joy cuffed both of Omar's wrists to each of the bedpost. "Now you are going to learn to obey my demands." Joy stood up on the bed looking down at Omar. "Let me show you what happens when I tell you to bring me, my dick and you don't." Joy now stood with each one of her feet close to Omar's ribcage in a straddling position. What she did next, not even Omar could believe.

Joy stared directly into Omar's eyes and then let a hot stream of urine splash down on his chest. "WHAT THE?" Omar screamed as he tried his best to wiggle away from the downpour that seemed to last forever. "BITCH, I'M GOING TO---"

"Going to what? What are you going to do, Omar?" Omar heard the voice, but his brain could not match it quickly enough. He knew one thing for certain that it wasn't Joy's voice. "Wave hi to the camera," Bria said stepping out of the walk-in closet holding her iPhone up.

Poor Omar looked back and forth from Bria to Joy in pure disbelief. He was too shocked to say a word. "Let me tell you exactly what you're going to do," Bria said in a serious manner. "First you are going to delete those photos that you have of me and Sugar and then you're going to break up with Tia in a way that she'll never forgive you, or else! Wait, before you make any sudden decisions, I can show you better than I can tell you."

Bria picked up the remote control and turned the flat screen on. The first images that Omar saw were of him getting the deepest, wettest, blowjob ever from Becky Nash. The next scene was of him fucking Joy faster than a rabbit and then last, but surely not least, he saw Joy urinating all over his chest. "Now, do we have a deal or what, Mr. Panty Ripper?"

There was no hesitation in Omar's reply, "Yeah, but you bitches just declared war with my heart."

"Yeah, yeah, yeah… Stop ya whining before I make her piss on you again," Bria said as her and Joy bust out laughing. Omar was mad, but he knew he would get the last laugh.

14 Chap

Heartbreaker

Tia walked into the restaurant with butterflies in her stomach. Omar had called her about an hour ago asking her to come to the restaurant A.S.A.P. In the back of her mind, she was extremely excited thinking that maybe he was about to pop the big question. *"I know my stuff is good, but I did not know it would only take one night to become Mrs. Tia Goodness,"* she thought as she turned the corner to the surprise of her life. Omar sat at the table casually dressed hugged up on Millie with absolutely no shade.

"What the fuck is all this?" Tia asked with enough attitude to cause some of the other guest to turn and look.

"Calm down. I---"

"NO! DON'T FUCKING TELL ME TO CALM DOWN!"

"Alright, well let me just keep it all the way real with you, Tia. I love both of y'all. Now Millie is willing to share. The question is, is you?"

Tia responded by picking up a half-filled glass of water and tossing it in Omar's face. With tears in her eyes, she parted with the coldest words that she had ever spoke.

"I WILL HATE YOU TIL THE DAY I DIE!"

Omar and Millie watched as Tia stormed out of the restaurant. Omar wanted to run after her and confess his loyalty to her and explain everything from beginning to end, but he couldn't. Millie's hand just so happened to ease over and squeeze his dick through his slacks. Omar gently slid her hand away.

"Now you know this was a favor and not a deal so let's not go there, Millie. I really need your help. Those two evil witches have ruined my future and you're going to help me make them pay."

Millie slid her hand back on Omar's dick. "You're right, Omar. This is a favor, but you know how to motivate me to give my best performance. Gas me up with this super unleaded and watch me crush those filthy animals!"

Once Again, It's On

For the past three days and nights, Millie got exactly what she had been asking for. Losing Tia again brought the beast out of Omar causing him to fuck Millie with an animalistic destruction and now it was her turn to uphold her end of the deal. Going after her ex-coworkers and friends did not bother her one bit. Millie only cared about what Millie wanted, bottom line!

Millie walked into her old job with her head held high. She had already talked to the boss who assured her that she could have her old position back so when she sat down at her cubical, Joy and Bria tried their best not to stare at her with gaping mouths.

Millie stepped right into character after arranging her desk. She grabbed a box of tissues, dabbed at the corner of her eyes, and sniffled loudly. Simultaneously, Joy and Bria rushed over to console her.

"Oh my God Millie, I don't know whether to welcome you back or hug you. Why are you crying?" Bria asked curiously as Joy stood by her with her lips twisted up and one of her eyebrows raised.

"I...I...really don't want to talk about it. I just need to get to work to keep my mind off of---" Millie blew her nose loudly. "I can't even say his name." Joy and Bria looked at each other. Bria shrugged her shoulders as if to say she didn't know whom Millie was talking about.

"What did "HE" do to you?" Bria asked now knowing what else to say.

"He told me that if I moved back here that he would marry me. I left my job, my home, and a healthy relationship, and then I get here and he tells me that he and his ex decided to give their relationship one last, *(SNIFFLE)* try. I hate him! I hate him so damn much!" Millie burst out into a loud sobbing cry that broke Bria's heart, but had little effect on Joy's suspicion.

To Joy, Millie was one of Omar's flings so there was absolutely no love or sympathy in her heart for Millie, at all!

"Who did this to you?" Bria pressed.

"That NO GOOD ASS OMAR GOODNESS and that sneaky fake ass goody two shoe Tia!" Millie spat. Bria wrapped her arms around her old friend.

"It's going to be okay. We hate Omar too," Bria honestly stated. If she only knew that it was Millie who had ruined her relationship with Tia by seducing Sugar and stealing the photos out of her phone and giving them to Omar. She would have rung Millie's neck right there on the job.

"Hate Omar? Speak for your damn self!" Joy thought as she watched Millie with an interrogating eye. "So why don't you go back, find your man, get a new job, house, and whatever else you lost, instead of staying here and being so close to the people that caused you this much pain and loss," Joy said in an even uncompassionate tone.

"No! What I'm going to do is work my butt off until I can afford to relocate. I'll just rent a room, *(SNIFFLE)* for the time being.

"Nonsense! You can stay with me until you get back on your feet," Bria offered falling right into Millie's trap.

"I don't know. Wouldn't your girlfriend have a problem with that?"

"Girl please! I've been single so long that I truly feel like a nun at times. It's just me and my best friend Apple staying at my place and you are more than welcome."

15 Chap

I'm In

"*O mar is going to be so proud of me,*" Millie thought as Bria led her into her home.

"APPLE! COME DOWNSTAIRS!" Bria screamed. "Can I get you something to drink?" she asked Millie.

"Yes, but please make it strong and hold the ice." Bria disappeared into the kitchen as Apple came down the stairs looking ghetto as hell with a hair scarf on her head and some Hello Kitty pajamas on. She looked Millie up and down and when she noticed her luggage, she blurted out, "OH HELL TO THE NIZZO!"

Apple stormed into the kitchen where she found Bria pouring two glasses of Cognac. "Where mine at?" Apple asked with an obvious attitude.

"I---"

"Don't think you gonna put me out."

"What? Girl, what the hell is you talking about?"

"What the hell is Millie doing here? I didn't know y'all was bumping twats."

"It's not what you think. Trust me," Bria said side stepping Apple and heading back to Millie who was now sitting on the leather sectional with her legs crossed. Bria handed her the drink.

"Thanks. I really needed this to calm my nerves."

"How long is you staying because it ain't enough food for three?" Apple asked walking into the room.

"Oh no, I'll be supporting myself. Keep your EBT card in your pocket." Millie's attempt to take a shot at Apple went unnoticed.

"Good! Cause I stretch my stamps out for the whole month. A bitch don't be in the supermarket making it rain. Hell no! No balling in the cereal aisle." Bria shook her head in embarrassment as Millie gulped down her drink. "I heard a rumor about you."

"Here we go," Millie thought. "Oh yeah? I hope it was good."

"Hell to the yeah! I heard that pussy taste like sweet buttermilk," Apple said licking her lips while letting her eyes drop down to Millie's camel toe.

"APPLE! Don't be rude! I'm sorry Millie. I apologize for my friend. She never bites her tongue."

"It's okay. I take it as a compliment.

"Let me show you the guest room," Apple said smiling.

"The guest room, Apple. Not your room!" Bria said in an, *I'm watching you* manner. She felt that Millie had recently been through a heart breaking, life-changing trauma due to Omar Goodness and the last thing she needed was Apple making advances towards what she thought was a distraught Mille. Boy was she wrong.

The Fella's

Kinard was on his third drink he had been sulking and complaining ever since the trio had entered the bar. "I'll do anything to get her back."

"Well you can start by letting a real man blow her back out, and you and she could just be BFF's," Askari joked, a little too loud for Kinard's liking. "Nah, I'm just playing. It's just hard to take this *supposed to be* relationship serious when we never met the girl. Shit, we don't even know her name."

"He do have a point," Omar chimed in and then took a swig of his drink.

"Well, that's because I didn't want you two womanizing perverts to mess things up for me," Kinard said while digging in his pocket and pulling out his phone. "Y'all actually already met her at Omar's party." He turned his phone around and showed them a picture of him and Joy. He was cheesing from ear to ear in the picture and she wasn't smiling at all. Omar's mouth fell wide open. "Her name is Joy and she was my world," Kinard said.

"That evil fucking bitch," Omar thought to himself. "Listen Bro." Omar's thoughts were interrupted by Askari's twisted logic. "The only way to get over a bitch is to get under another one."

"JOY IS NOT A BITCH!" Kinard yelled and shot to his feet and stormed out of the bar.

Frustration

Omar sat behind his desk trying his best to go over the new marketing proposition for a Goodies sex toy line, but his anger with Joy consumed his every thought. So he decided to call her phone. She picked up on the first ring and he let her have it. "You sneaky, cold hearted bitch! I should come over there and kick your high yellow ass! You intentionally made my best friend love you knowing that he is weak and you crushed his heart and ego!"

Omar's rant was cut short by the sound of Joy giggling in the background and then a CLICK! The phone went dead in Omar's ear further pissing him off. He slammed his phone down on his desk hard causing Becky to gasp and step back. She walked in and was too turned on by his aggressive roar to interrupt.

"I...I...I'm sorry, My Lord."

"What do you want Becky?" Omar asked with an obvious attitude.

"Only to worship your every demand."

"Cut the shit, Becky! All I want to do is kick some ass, right about now!"

"Your wishes is the only law that I live by." Becky locked the office door, walked over to Omar's desk, and hiked her skirt up to her waist exposing the fact that she wore no panties.

"What the hell are you doing? We're not having sex Becky!"

"I know My Lord. You said all you wanted to do was kick some ass, so take your shoe and sock off and release your frustration." Omar could not believe his ears. Becky wanted him to actually kick her in the ass. "Come on Omar, kick that bitch ass! Come on motherfucker! Like, totally make that bitch respect you, My Lord!"

"Becky, I'm not ---"

"The hell you are! Do it for your best friend that got his heart broke! I BROKE HIS HEART OMAR! I BROKE HIS HEART!" she yelled.

In a frantic hurry, Omar bent down and removed his right shoe and sock. "Alright, you asked for it and now you're going to get it!" Omar backed up to the rear wall while Becky took one hand off of the desk and slipped it between her legs. She started to finger her clit and then yelled, "I BROKE HIS HEART AND I LOVED IT! NOW WHAT ARE YOU GOING TO DO ABOUT IT?"

Omar ran towards her as if he was about to kick a field goal. WHACK!

Becky's whole body jerked and her ass stung like hell, but she loved the feeling and the fact that she was sacrificing her body, well her ass, to her

Lord. "What was that; a warm up? You better kick her ass good!"

This time Omar backed up to the side wall and came from an angle with a force that caused Becky to yelp out loud and cum all over her fingers. With a teeth chattering voice, Becky said, "That's right! Kick her ass, My Lord! Break your foot off up in that bitch ass!"

Omar didn't back up again. This time he dropped his pants and roughly entered Becky's soaking wet pink cunt.

16Chap

Rebound Chick

"I told you, all men are the same and that's why I'm a full fledge lesbian. I promise you, I can be everything you ever wanted in a friend, a partner, a lover, and whatever else you need me to be. But, you are going to have to prove to me that you won't go running back to Omar, and you won't scream his name in the middle of me pleasing you."

"Bria, I've apologized a million times for that. It was the damn strap on that threw me off. Trust me, me and Omar are done forever!"

"No, you have to be done with all men. You have to be in a one hundred percent committed relationship with me or I'm done," Bria said looking Tia straight in the eyes.

"Okay, I'll do it. From this moment on, I'm done with men and I promise to give you my all."

"Well, it's official then. Meet me in the shower." Bria walked into the bathroom, looked over her shoulder, and sent Omar a text.

Brianna 11:45

Destroy the pictures of me and Sugar or else your best friend Kinard will receive the sex tape of you and Joy! LMAO!

Candy Apple

Meanwhile back at Bria's house where she had left Apple and Millie so she could spend time with Tia. Apple was going harder than an iron trying to get inside of Millie's boy shorts. "Damn baby, why are you acting like that? I just want to kiss on it," Apple said as she squeezed on Millie's camel toe. Apple was not Millie's target so giving in to her advances was not going to happen. "Damn! It's so fat! Let me put some duck sauce on it, Millie."

Millie burst out laughing. "Girl, you are a trip. Look, I'm flattered and all, but my heart is still healing and sex is the last thing on my mind right now. I'm sorry."

"Alright, I guess I could understand that," Apple said with disappointment in her tone. "Well, can I at least smell it?" she begged.

Millie shook her head with a, *girl you are off the hook* smile on her face. Then she got up off the couch and said, "Goodnight Apple. I'm going to bed."

Apple got on her knees and smashed her face into the couch where Millie was just sitting and sniffed. "Ummmmmmm!"

All Millie could do was watch and think, *"Damn, these lesbians are worse than men."*

Millie walked up the stairs and instead of going into the guest room; she slipped inside of Bria's room and grabbed the iPad that was sitting on Bria's desk. Then she slid out of Bria's room and into her room. Millie pulled out the private investigators card that Omar had given her earlier that day and dialed his number.

"Mr. Knox, hey it's me, Millie. I have the iPad. Now you are going to have to walk me through this."

Forty-five minutes later, Millie had successfully hacked into Bria's iPad and emailed everything in it to Mr. Knox. When she was done, she snuck the iPad back into Bria's room and on her way back to the guest room, she passed by Apple's door which was slightly ajar. Millie could hear grunts and flesh smacking so out of curiosity, she tiptoed to the door and peeked inside.

"WHO PUSSY IS THIS?" a big bulldogger who resembled the rapper Gucci Man wearing a horse dick strap-on asked.

"IT'S YOURS KILO! OOOOOH KILO! IT'S YOURS!" Apple screamed as the stench hit Millie's nose almost causing her to puke. Millie ran back to the guest room pinching her nose with one hand and covering her mouth with the other.

Pray For Me

Omar sat in the first row at the First Baptist Church. He silently begged the Lord for forgiveness. Not being able to control his lustful sins has destroyed a good woman's faith in love. He also asked the Lord to forgive him for now taking vengeance into his own hands. Omar saw Sister Beatrice coming his way and he broke down with a loud sob.

Sister Beatrice patted his back and said, "Let it out son. Let the Lord take that pain away and turn it into a blessing." Sister Beatrice looked over her spectacles and said, "Did anyone ever tell you that you resemble that young millionaire. What's his name? Omar…Omar Goodies? The one that makes the lingerie."

Omar wiped away the invisible tears. "It's Omar Goodness," he said and then reached his hand out for Sister Beatrice to shake it. Her whole body began to shake. A millionaire in her presence seemed to give her body the Holy Ghost. Sister Beatrice fell into Omar's lap and began to speak in tongues. Omar who was somewhat in shock did the only logical thing he could do. He grabbed the paper fan off of the bench and fanned Sister Beatrice's face.

In return, Sister Beatrice discreetly squeezed his dick through his slacks. Now Omar had heard the rumors of Sister Beatrice being a coldblooded freak, but never would he have guessed that she would literally throw herself on him in the middle of

Sunday's sermon. Sister Beatrice was one of those mid-forties women who could still pass for a woman in her late twenties. So needless to say, Omar Goodness fell victim right there in the house of the Lord as he fanned her with one hand and discreetly used his other hand to pinch her nipple through her thin summer dress. So yeah, Omar came to the church to ask the Lord for forgiveness and he left with Sister Beatrice. He took it as a sign of being forgiven.

17 Chap

Becky's Home

O mar rang Becky's doorbell twice before she came and opened the door. Her heart skipped a beat when she saw her God standing there. His unannounced visit made her moist in an instant. Becky ripped her while blouse off of her back with buttons flying everywhere. Omar looked at her like she was crazy, but when she laid the blouse over the welcome mat, he understood her clearly. Omar entered, but stopped to wipe his Gucci loafers on the blouse.

"You may enter, My Lord."

This whole godly thing was starting to grow on Omar. He even spoke in what he figured was a Godly tone.

"Come wash thy cock and body. I reek of Sister Beatrice feminine juices and cream."

"Yes, My Lord." For the next forty-five minutes, Becky washed every inch of Omar Goodness from head to toe. When she was done, she dried him off and tucked him in. Omar lay flat on his stomach as Becky massaged him into a deep sleep. White women gotta love them!

Please Don't

Omar was awaken by the constant ringing of the doorbell. He looked over at Becky who was in a deep sleep. After a loud sigh, he got up and headed to the door in his silk boxers. *"This better not be Millie,"* he thought as he swung the door open. Omar was surprised to see his best friend Kinard standing there soaking wet from the rain. "Hey Bro, what's going on?" Omar asked. After he didn't get a response, Omar asked, "Are you okay? What the --"

"What is this, Omar?" Kinard raised his hand and passed Omar his phone. Omar looked down at the screen and saw himself fucking Joy in the ass. He heard Kinard sniffle. When he looked up in an attempt to apologize, Omar found himself staring down the barrel of a gun.

"WHOA!" Omar screamed as he began to back up. "KINARD, WHAT ---"

"SHUT THE FUCK UP!" Kinard screamed like a madman. "I LOVED HER...AND YOU KNEW IT!" *SNIFFLE* "YOU DIRTY SON-OF-A-BITCH! I HATE YOU!"

"KIN---"

BOOM! The first slug ripped through Omar's shoulder.

"AAAAHHHHHHHH!" Omar fell on his back and tried his best to scurry away, but Kinard walked up to him and pointed the gun at his chest. "PLEASE DON'T!"

BOOM!

Omar shot upright in Becky's bed with his heart beating a million miles a minute.

"Are you okay, My Lord?" Becky asked full of concern as she wiped the sweat from his forehead.

"Yeah…yeah…Just a bad dream. Go back to sleep." Omar could not go back to sleep after his nightmare. *"Damn, Kinard cannot see that tape, by any means, "* Omar thought to himself.

Edward Knox

Omar walked into the private investigators office with high hopes. Mr. Knox called Omar to his office with an urgency in his voice. The two men shook hands firmly. "Have a seat, Mr. Goodness."

Mr. Knox's professional demeanor gave Omar confidence that he had indeed found something useful on Bria's computer. "There's a few things that I'm sure you will find of interest, but this here trumps them all." Mr. Knox turned the laptop around so Omar could see it. There was two pictures. One of the pictures was of a teenage boy with the name BRIAN JONES as the heading and the other one was a picture of Bria with the heading BRIANNA JONES. It was obvious to Omar that Bria had a younger brother, but Omar didn't see the relevancy.

"And this is important...Why?" Omar said with frustration in his tone.

Edward Knox smiled and then said, "This is why." He clicked the mouse and what Omar saw next on the screen almost knocked him out of his seat. Omar jumped out of his seat and ran out of the private investigators office without so much as a glance back.

Tia's

Tia laid in Bria's arms with one thing, and only one thing on her mind…Omar! Something within her soul told her that something wasn't right about him and Millie being a couple. *"She must be holding something over his head. Yeah, that has to be it,"* Tia thought to herself.

"Tia…Tia…Tia! Girl, do you hear me talking to you?"

"Oh, Oh, I'm sorry. I must have dozed off," she lied.

"Well, I was saying that I love you," Bria whispered sweetly in her ear.

"Thank you."

"THANK YOU?" Bria screamed. "WHAT THE HELL EVER HAPPENED TO, I LOVE YOU TOO?"

"Please Bria. I'm going through a lot emotionally. I need you to help me get through this, not add to my stress!" Tia snapped.

"Don't tell me you sitting in here all salty over a man that does not want to be with you. You know what, I'm leaving. Call me whenever you get through whatever it is that you are going through."

"No! Please don't leave me too," she cried. Bria grabbed her things and with a sad look on her face she said, "You have to get yourself together. Dude got you tripping."

Bria left the house, leaving a teary-eyed Tia, heartbroken and all alone. Tia sent Omar a text.

Can you talk?

After twenty minutes and no response from Omar, Tia threw her phone against the wall smashing it into pieces.

18 Chap

God Giveth

Omar and Becky stepped off the private elevator on the 19th floor of Omar's condo apartment building. They both were past the point of intoxication as they stumbled into the apartment. Omar was in a celebratory mood, now that he *felt* like he had gained the upper hand on the situation that had caused him to lose sleep for the last two weeks. He knew that his chances of getting Tia back was slim to none so now his new mission in life was to crush Bria and Joy's souls.

Omar led Becky to the balcony that over looked the nightlife of the city. "Wow My Lord, this is a magnificent view." Omar walked up to Becky and slid her dress off of her shoulders causing it to fall to the floor. She was wearing a silk bra and panty set by Goodies. Omar unhooked the bra and tossed it over the balcony. The cool night air caused her pink nipples to stiffen instantly.

"Are you afraid of heights?"

"A little," Becky said and then looked down the nineteen stories to the ground. "Good." With the strength of a weight lifter, Omar scooped Becky up and stood her up on the eight-inch wide ledge. A scream was stuck somewhere in the back of

Becky's throat. Maybe if she weren't so tipsy, she wouldn't have been so nervous.

Omar grabbed her ankles, looked up at her, and said, "Squat down."

With wobbly legs, Becky did what she was told. This placed her cunt parallel to Omar's face. "Hold on to my shoulders." Becky's heart skipped a beat when she realized what was about to happen. Omar had never orally pleased her, up until this point, but that was about to change. She didn't have a clue that he was about to do what he did.

Omar snapped his teeth at her silk panties causing her to flinch. "Don't move," he demanded and then snapped and snapped again until he caught a piece of the fabric in between his teeth and then he began to forcefully tug at it until it began to tear.

"Holy crap! Holy crap!" Becky whispered as Omar used his teeth to rip her silk panties completely off. Omar locked his lips around Becky's swollen pink clit and with the speed of a professional; he twirled the tip of his tongue pressing her button in. "OOOH FUUUUCCCKKK!" she screamed. "OOOH YEAH! RIGHT THERE! RIGHT THERE! OH, I'LL CUM! I'LL CUM!" Becky's body began to tremble as she dug her nails into Omar's shoulders and exploded all down his chin.

Becky was literally seeing stars as she howled up to the moon. Little did she know that this was only the beginning. Next, Omar held her hands and turned her around to face the city. Becky was still in her squatting position with her ass now in Omar's face.

Omar being the animal that he was, spit in the crack of Becky's ass and then stuck his tongue inside of it, which caught her off guard. This caused her to flinch up onto her tippy toes. "OOOOOHHHHHHHHHH...UMMMM...OOH... FUUUCCCCCK!" Omar slid two fingers inside of her dripping wet cunt and sent her into yet another orgasm. Becky's brain turned into noodles as she began to lean forward. Using his free hand, Omar grabbed her by her ponytail and pulled her back to safety which only caused her to gush all over his hand.

After fifteen seconds of convulsions, Omar turned her back around to face him. He grabbed her ankles and blew cool air on her clit. "FUUUCCCCK! I can't...I can't take it anymore, My Lord!" Omar ignored her pleas and nosedived back into her pool. "UMMMM...MMM...MMM!" Becky began to feel light headed as she felt herself quickly building up. "O...OMAR! I...I......CAN'T HOLD ON! I'MMA LIKE, TOTALLY, TOTALLY CUM!" Her confession only motivated him to go faster as he slurped loudly on her cunt.

If his face were not buried so deep, he would have been able to see her eyes rolling in the back of her head. Omar did feel her hands slide off of his shoulders. Becky began to drool down on the back of his neck, which caused Omar to look up just in time. Her mouth made the letter "O" as she began to fall backwards in what seemed to Omar like slow motion. Still holding her ankles tightly, gravity took her downward.

"WHOA! WHOA! I GOT YOU! JUST HOLD ON!" Omar screamed as Becky hung upside down from the 19th floor. Little did Omar know that Becky was no longer conscience. She had blacked out. Her body began to shake violently and then the strangest thing ever happened. Becky began to squirt with so much force that it was literally splashing in Omar's face and eyes.

"I CAN'T SEE! I CAN'T SEE!" he screamed frantically

The Next Day

Omar could not breathe without Becky blocking his air passageway. She was officially turned the hell out. The fact that his tongue game almost killed her only excited her that much more. "Is there anything else that I can get you or do for you, My Lord?" she asked from his office doorway.

Omar licked his lips in a non-seductive manner and Becky almost creamed on herself. "No, and I'm Mr. Goodness at work. Now go before I have to spank that ass until it turns red," Omar said with a smirk and a wink.

"Are you threatening me with a good time, Mr. Goodness?" Becky crooned as she backed out of his office. Becky was slowly, but surely beginning to grow on Omar, but unlike her Omar was totally shaken by the fact that she could have died the night before. *"What the hell was I thinking,"* he thought right before he heard a loud commotion outside of his office. Omar rushed to see what it was and what he found was Becky in a headlock that Millie had executed effortlessly.

"MILLIE! TAKE YOUR HANDS OFF OF HER!"

"No! This bitch smacked me and I'm going to whoop her skinny ass!"

"You slapped her?" Omar asked in somewhat disbelief.

"Yes, My Lord, she ---"

"MY LORD? WHAT THE?" Millie asked in confusion.

"Let her go Millie!"

Millie released Becky, pushed her out of her way, walked up to Omar, and kissed him on his lips. "So this is what you do when you are at work? Do you ever give this dick a rest?" She grabbed his dick through his slacks while looking him in his eyes seductively and it only took a few seconds of this before Becky went ape shit! She charged at Millie like a bull.

"GET THE HELL OFF OF IT, WHORE!" Millie sidestepped Becky's weak attempt and tossed her over Omar's secretary's desk causing all of the contents to crash to the floor right along with Becky. Millie politely returned to her conversation as if nothing had even happened.

"Like I was saying before I was rudely interrupted. Whatever you are planning, you need to make it happen like yesterday."

"And why is that?" Omar questioned.

"Because Bria got Tia's head on an emotional rollercoaster. The sad part about it is that I'm sure Bria is not interested in Tia any longer. She's just mentally abusing her because she left her to be with you.

Becky stood to her feet huffing and puffing looking as if she was about to charge Millie again.

"Becky sit down," Omar said in an even tone without even looking at her.

"Yes, My Lord," Becky replied without even another thought as she sat down quietly.

Millie chuckled, "Damn! That dick is powerful around here, I see."

Omar ignored Millie's sarcasm and introduced the two ladies. "Millie this is Becky. Becky this is Millie and I'm going to need you two to get along."

"As long as she don't mind sharing that dick," Millie said and then turned to Becky. "Do you?" Becky looked at Omar with pleading eyes, but Omar just stared her down and asked," Well, do you?"

"No, My Lord. Your pleasure is my only mission in life."

"Good! Now the two of you come over here and kiss and make up." Without absolutely no apprehension, Becky walked up to Millie and stuck her tongue down her throat. Omar sat back and observed the two ladies as they moaned and sucked all over each other's lips. Omar led them into his office, dropped his slacks, pulled his dick out, and then told the two freaks to share! They both dropped to their knees and fifteen seconds later, there was an explosion.

Turning the Tables

Bria rushed to Tia's home after receiving an urgent message from Tia telling her to come to her house ASAP. Bria rang the doorbell at a rapid pace until Tia opened the door looking beautiful as usual. Bria walked into the house and the first thing she noticed was OMAR GOODNESS sitting on the leather sectional with a glass of champagne in his hand looking like the world was his. Bria turned to Tia with an attitude and asked, "What is all of this?" She was referring to Omar.

"Come sit down," Tia said grabbing Bria by the hand, walking her over to the couch, and sitting her down. "First, let me say that I'm surprised at the both of you. Omar explained to me everything that you both did to win my affection. I guess y'all did not realize the pain that each of those actions caused me. I just want to know if there's any more secrets that I should know about from either of you."

"I've told you everything, as far as me. Maybe Bria would like to confess about some things." Bria looked at Omar and asked, "Did you tell her about your white girl?"

"Yeah, he told me about Becky and how you and Joy got him on camera and blackmailed him for Joy's own sexual gratification, but what about you Bria? Is there something you think you should have told me in the beginning about our relationship?" Bria sat with a confused look on her face.

"In the beginning? Tia, I have told you my whole life story, so whatever mind games Omar is playing with you, I ---"

"MIND GAMES?" Omar yelled picking up his iPhone and pressing some buttons on the screen. Then he handed it to Bria. Bria saw the images on the phone and immediately began to feel dizzy. She dropped the phone to the floor, covered her mouth, and began to back away from Omar and Tia. Omar picked up the phone and then spoke directly to Bria, "Brianna Jones, or should I say Brian Jones?"

"Bria, how could you not tell me that you were born a man?" Tia asked wiping tears from her eyes.

"If I ever see you in this town again Brian, I'll make sure you little secret goes viral," Omar threatened. Bria shook her head like an afraid child and then ran out of Tia's apartment without uttering a word or even looking back. Tia felt bad for her, but Omar on the other hand, loved every second of it for all the hell that her and Joy had put him through.

19Chap

Speaking In Tongue

Omar got to Joy's house two hours later after she had demanded for him to be there within the next thirty minutes. She was pissed to the tenth power and Omar had the nerve to stroll in all calm and cool with his swagger on a billion. "What the hell took you so long? Get upstairs now and strip naked! I'm going to have to whip some discipline into my slave!" Omar chuckled at Joys' statements and proceeded to climb the stairs.

Once he was inside the bedroom, Omar flipped the script. He walked over to Joy's dresser, removed the handcuffs, and tucked them inside of his back pocket. "So you do like being cuffed and pissed on, huh?" Joy asked. Omar walked up to Joy and grabbed her by the throat lifting her up off of her feet. He could see it in her eyes that she was turned on by his aggressiveness. Omar slammed her down on the soft bed causing her body to bounce on impact. "Oh my God, Omar! You got it soaking wet!"

"Shut your little freak ass up," Omar said while he roughly grabbed Joy's wrist and slapped one of the cuffs on her wrist, the same way police officers do criminals.

"So now you are going to piss on me, Omar? Well, go ahead then! I'll love every drop of it, you big dick son-of-a-bitch!" Omar was tired of hearing Joy's mouth so he grabbed at her lace panties and ripped them off without his normal seduction. Next, he used those ripped panties to gag her. Then he yanked her cuffed hand over to the bedpost and cuffed her to it.

"The games stop now, Joy! You had your fun and now it's time for me to have mine!" Omar wheeled the TV stand to the foot of the bed so she could get a clear unobstructed view. "I mean, how long did you think this sex slaving thing would go on before I figured out a way to stick it back to you?"

"OOOH YES! Stick it back to me," Joy moaned and squeezed her thighs tightly together. Omar just ignored her.

"Now, I'm going to give you a choice. Either you go crawling back to Kinard on your hands and knees, begging him to marry you or ---"

Omar cut his sentence off and put a disc in the DVD player, pressed play, and walked out of Joy's bedroom without looking back. By the time he reached his car, he could hear Joy scream all kind of vulgar obscenities.

Joy stopped her tantrum and starred at the images on the screen. Sister Beatrice was splashing Holy Water on Omar's dick and then sucking it off with a skill that put Superhead to shame! Joy had to control herself from getting turned on, but GOOD GOD! Was Sister Beatrice doing the damn thing and what she did next proved that there is no age limit when it comes to a certified freak!

Sister Beatrice removed Omar's dick from her wet mouth, lifted his leg up just enough to give her some leverage, and then licked his asshole as if she was possessed by the devil, all the while jerking his saliva-drenched dick at the same time. Sister Beatrice had Omar moaning like a little bitch as she began to literally speak in tongues in between flicking her tongue insanely fast.

"OH SHIT! OH SHIT! HERE IT COMES...ARRRRRRGGH!" Omar screamed and then shot his load straight up in the air. It came down with a, *SPLAT*. Just like bird crap does when it falls on the top of someone's car. It fell right on the top of Sister Beatrice favorite straw church hat and then dripped down onto her forehead, nose, and upper lip, which she gladly licked off and swallowed like the freak she was. Joy screamed, reached for her phone with her free hand, and dialed a number. The phone rang twice and then it was answered.

"Praise the Lord, Sister Beatrice speaking."

"MOTHER!" Joy screamed at the top of her lungs. "YOU FUCKING WHORE!"

20 Chap

Tug Of War

Six months had passed since Omar Goodness had taken back control of his life. Bria, well Brian, had left town and never returned. Joy was four months pregnant by Kinard and their wedding date was set for June. They both seemed to be ecstatic about everything going on in their lives. Millie and Becky were both living with Omar trying to outdo each other with every little thing, especially anything sexual. Omar was not complaining, but at times their competiveness got on his last damn nerve and this particular morning was no different.

"How is your orange juice, My Lord?" Becky asked as the trio sat eating the breakfast that both women had prepared.

"It's fine."

"Well it's like totally freshly squeezed. I did it myself," Becky said.

Millie rolled her eyes. "How are your eggs? Are they cheesy enough, Omar?"

"They are perfect, Millie."

"I know that's right. You know black people know how to season their food."

"Hey! Don't be a racist," Becky joked.

"How can I be a racist when you know I love that white pussy?" Millie leaned over and began to suck on Becky's bottom lip. This was the little games that they played to turn Omar on so he could pound their sweet spots. Omar was just about to join in when he heard the doorbell.

"Who the hell? It's nine o'clock on a Sunday morning," Omar said standing up wearing only his robe and walking over to the door to open it. Millie and Becky got up, walked right over, and stood behind him. When Omar opened the door, to their surprise Tia stood on the other side of the door looking as if she had just dropped from Heaven. Millie's blood pressure went straight to the roof. Becky's cheeks turned beet red, and Omar's heart skipped a few beats. "Tia, what brings you here? I haven't seen you for months. Is everything okay?" he rambled.

"Actually, everything is just fine. The queen is back to claim her throne."

Omar was at a loss for words, but the Kool-Aid smile on his face spoke volumes. Tia looked over his shoulders at Becky and Millie's nervous reactions. "Don't worry ladies, y'all can stay. A king will always need his toys to play with. Just know your place," Tia said with the straightest face ever. "Now you two can get my luggage from the car while me and the king go upstairs and get reacquainted."

Millie and Becky both looked at Tia as if she had lost her damn mind and then they looked at Omar like, *"Put this bitch in her place!"* The smile on Omar's face disappeared instantly. He turned to Becky and Millie and said, "The queen has spoken. Now get the royal luggage from the car."

Tia walked up to Omar, shoved her sweet tongue down his throat, grabbed his hand, and led him up to the master bedroom. Millie and Becky silently did as they were told, but all the while thinking about different ways to get Tia out of the picture. *"Oh she just started a war! Let the best bitch or bitches win!"* the two ladies thought to themselves.

To Be Continued...

Books by Good2Go Authors on Our Bookshelf

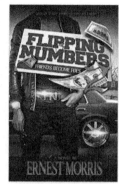

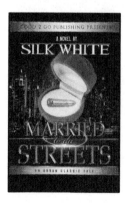

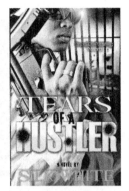

Good2Go Films Presents

To order books, please fill out the order form below:

To order films please go to www.good2gofilms.com

Name:_____

Address:_____

City: _____ State: _____ Zip Code: _____

Phone:_____

Email:_____

Method of Payment: Check   VISA   MASTERCARD

Credit Card#:_____

Name as it appears on card: _____

Signature: _____

Item Name	Price	Qty	Amount
48 Hours to Die – Silk White	$14.99		
Flipping Numbers – Ernest Morris	$14.99		
He Loves Me, He Loves You Not - Mychea	$14.99		
He Loves Me, He Loves You Not 2 - Mychea	$14.99		
He Loves Me, He Loves You Not 3 - Mychea	$14.99		
Married To Da Streets – Silk White	$14.99		
My Boyfriend's Wife - Mychea	$14.99		
Never Be The Same – Silk White	$14.99		
Stranded – Silk White	$14.99		
Slumped – Jason Brent	$14.99		
Tears of a Hustler - Silk White	$14.99		
Tears of a Hustler 2 - Silk White	$14.99		
Tears of a Hustler 3 - Silk White	$14.99		
Tears of a Hustler 4- Silk White	$14.99		
Tears of a Hustler 5 – Silk White	$14.99		
Tears of a Hustler 6 – Silk White	$14.99		
The Panty Ripper - Reality Way	$14.99		
The Panty Ripper 2 – Reality Way	$14.99		
The Teflon Queen – Silk White	$14.99		
The Teflon Queen 2 – Silk White	$14.99		
The Teflon Queen 3 – Silk White	$14.99		
The Teflon Queen 4 – Silk White	$14.99		
Time Is Money - Silk White	$14.99		
Young Goonz – Reality Way	$14.99		
Subtotal:			
Tax:			
Shipping (Free) U.S. Media Mail:			
Total:			

Make Checks Payable To: Good2Go Publishing - 7311 W Glass Lane, Laveen, AZ 85339